RAJA AND THE THRONE OF ZURKIA

VOLUME I

AVAH BROC

FriesenPress

Suite 300 - 990 Fort St
Victoria, BC, V8V 3K2
Canada

www.friesenpress.com

First Edition — 2019

ISBN
978-1-5255-3245-0 (Hardcover)
978-1-5255-3246-7 (Paperback)
978-1-5255-3247-4 (eBook)

1. *Fiction, Fantasy, Historical*

Distributed to the trade by The Ingram Book Company

LAND OF ROUSSE
WSYRUT
Skyep Sea
YURX ISLAND
NORTH VEL SACA
ZURKIA
VOLGA RIVER
ZURKIA
KAZANKA RIVER
ODYHUN
PAVEL'S ESTATE
BOLGER
PORT ALEXANDRA
MANOR
KAZAN
DEMARCUS
VOLGA RIVER
ZURKIA
VOZANE RIVER
MARSH
VALETTA
SOUTH VEL SACA
DRACON
YURPHYN RIVER
FETHERLAND
DESERT
BAKU
PORT CAPHANNE
KULALY ISLAND
Khvalyn Sea

N

Table of Contents

Part I

The Peasant Girl

Chapter I

The Young Lord

The young lord rode his palfrey along the cut fields of grass. He now sat almost as tall as his father. His wavy black hair fell on his broadening shoulders. He wore knee-high leather boots and a brown cape that draped over his saddle.

Scanning the fields for any disturbances, he found the patterned terrain reminded him of the woven rugs he saw in the bazaars of Kazan. He marveled at how the peasants so precisely created the worked strips of land. In the distance, he heard singing as the men swung their scythes in unison.

The nearby portions of fields were ready to harvest, so workers were in close proximity. Pavel watched the men gather the cut grass with their wooden rakes. Then, while he was looking just ahead, he noticed a commotion.

A man and a young girl were working closely together. He could hear the man speaking gruffly to the girl. Pavel motioned his horse closer to them.

"Get working!" said the man.

"My rake is broken," said the girl.

The man took the rake and threw it aside.

The girl's face looked strained and tired. Dirt covered her skin, which made it difficult to tell her age. Her look was somewhat intense, yet there was a childlike softness in her face. She was fairly tall but her slight frame made her look young. She wore a wimple on her head that was held in place by a black band. The simple scarf covered her hair and neck, but strands of hair had come free and stuck to her face.

The girl wore a white gathered blouse. It had streaks of dirt on it and was tucked into her tattered, woolen, gray skirt. A wide sash was wrapped tightly around her waist. Although her skirt was long, her feet were still exposed, revealing that she was not wearing any footwear.

"Get down on your knees and use your hands," said the man.

The girl did as she was told. The cut stalks of grass were rough, and the sharp edges had already cut the skin on her feet. As the girl crawled along, gathering grass, the short stalks punctured her knees. She winced at the pain and stood up again, but the man poked her with his rake and told her to get back down on her hands and knees.

Pavel didn't know which feeling was stronger, anger or compassion. He wanted to haul the man onto the road and beat him, but his father's mentoring prevented him from doing that. They all struggled, all the peasants. It was fear that motivated them—fear of not producing enough for their lord, fear of the future for their family. Their lives were not their own. They were owned, but protection from outside invaders is what kept them in the village.

Pavel's father, Lord Ramazon, was a good man. He had been given the Royal Order of Archanglim by the Tzarina of Zurkia for his heroism in protecting her against a raid while she was on route. His reputation throughout Zurkia earned him respect from royals and peasants alike. On his own estate he treated the peasants with kindness. Pavel had been taught to be firm with the peasants, but without harshness. He would settle this situation calmly and logically.

He used his legs to move his horse right up to the man and girl. They continued to gather the grass and did not look up.

"What's going on here?" asked Pavel. "Why isn't this girl with the younger women?"

The other peasants who were not that far away stopped their work to watch.

The man dropped his rake and turned to face Pavel. "I have been working the lord's plot of land and do not have enough time to work my own. I must use my daughter's help, so I can pay the dowry that is expected for her."

"A dowry, you say?"

"Yes, it is for my only daughter and child," said the man. "She has been given permission to marry someone in Lord Lythym's village. I am afraid I will not have enough for the dowry, so she needs to help me."

"Why is it so urgent?" asked Pavel.

"The time is short. And I need to teach her to work hard so she will not be cast out of her new family."

Pavel looked at the girl. She somehow seemed different; she did not possess the usual peasantry traits he was accustomed to. "I'm sure she already knows how to work hard."

The man stuttered as he answered. "Yes . . . yes, she already knows how to work hard, but . . . but . . . I must obtain enough for a dowry."

"This is no way to treat a young daughter," said Pavel. "I don't see why the situation is so urgent. I am surprised she has not run away with this type of treatment."

Pavel knew that peasants who ran away would not be accepted in another village, and usually did not live long from lack of food or from being brutally treated. He didn't want this happening to this girl. He quickly contemplated the situation and spoke again. "This girl is much too young to be married. I will release you from this burden of obtaining a dowry. Your daughter will come with me."

"Please," said the man as he dropped to his knees. "The family my daughter is to marry into has promised us two goats. But if you take my daughter, my wife and I will be shamed. They will come and take the one goat that we have."

"I will see to it that you will have more goats," said Pavel. "My father is generous with the villagers. This is not an excuse to be doing this to your daughter. You seem overly harsh with her."

Pavel spoke kindly to the girl. "Stand up and come here."

The girl stood. She was even taller than he expected. A glimmer of fear showed in her eyes as she looked at Pavel. She quickly lowered her face, staring at the ground.

"Don't be afraid. I will not harm you. Come over to my horse."

The girl walked toward Pavel with slow, small steps.

Commanding the girl's father, he said, "Help your daughter onto my horse. She can ride behind me."

The father meekly walked over to Pavel's horse and with trembling arms helped his daughter onto the back of the horse.

Turning his horse in a full circle, Pavel said, "Hang onto my waist tightly."

Not having any other choice, the girl wrapped her arms around Pavel. Then, almost instantly, Pavel motioned his horse into a full gallop toward his father's manor.

The manor could be seen in the distance; a long, two-story building displaying rows of windows stood out on the hill. At each end of the front of the building, additional long buildings stretched out toward the back and were joined with a wall of stone. The corners of the manor were fortified with rounded towers topped with parapets.

The keep tower stood in the center courtyard of the manor. A bell sounded with three clangs from the top of the keep signaling the young lord's approach.

Pavel's horse trotted across the stone walkway that was built over the wide moat. He then slowed his horse to cross the drawbridge.

As Pavel arrived at the manor, the servants surrounded him. They helped the girl down. Pavel jumped from his horse and then a few servants took it to the stables of the outer court.

Pavel gave orders to the rest of the servants. "Take this girl and see to it that all her needs are met. Give her some rest. Then put her in proper work clothes and teach her how to be a servant in my father's manor. She will dine with us in two months' time."

The girl was whisked away with the maids. She could do nothing but consent to their wishes.

Whispers surrounded her as the servants wondered who she was, and why the lord's son would want to seize a ragged peasant girl and have her occupy the halls of the manor.

Chapter 2

Concealed Visitor

"What's your name?" asked Galina, who was one of the chambermaids. Raja had been taken to the second floor of the manor and into one of the larger chambers. Maids were busy making a place for her to sleep. It was going to be her very own chamber.

"My name is Raja."

"Mmm, I haven't heard that name before. What does it mean?"

"Hope."

"Well now, how did you know that?"

"From the village storyteller."

"The village storyteller, you say. He is a wise one. How old are you?"

"Thirteen."

"Well, I wouldn't have guessed that according to your height," said Galina. "How did you get so tall?"

Raja said nothing.

Galina fastened the girdle around Raja's brown dress and then draped a shawl over her. Raja's hair, now washed, hung in tangled strands down her back. Galina worked to untangle it.

"I have never seen such long hair before. And the color golden red, where did that come from?"

Raja again said nothing.

"What's the matter? Can't you talk anymore?" asked Galina.

"I have no answers. My parents do not tell me anything about themselves, nor of their past."

"Your parents do not tell you anything?" asked Galina.

"No."

"That's a bit strange, but it doesn't matter."

"Why not?"

"Your parents do not exist for you anymore. Now you belong here. You belong to the lord of the manor and his family." Galina pulled a comb through Raja's hair.

"What is to become of me here?" asked Raja. Oddly, there seemed to be a confidence in her voice. She spoke as if she knew she was somehow meant to be at the manor.

"Instead of being a peasant outside, you will now be a peasant inside."

"But am I now free?"

Galina was silent for a moment. "No," she said, with a slight heaviness in her voice. "We are still owned by the nobles."

Raja knew that she felt the same way as Galina.

"But it is a better life to work in the manor, not as harsh, and you have protection from the sun," said Galina.

"My destiny—it has changed, hasn't it?"

"Yes, but you must always remember to obey for things to stay good."

"I will," said Raja. "I will obey your every word."

"Good. You can rest now. Everything is here that you need for the night and food will be brought to you. You will start your training tomorrow."

"Before you leave, may I ask what your name is?"

"Galina Gyden."

"I like you."

Raja thought there was a little smile on Galina's face as she left the room. Feeling tired, she climbed up on the stone bed that was attached to the wall. She lay there, but did not cry. Instead, she looked at the fire that burned in the fireplace, contemplating what had just happened. She wasn't sure if she would miss her parents. Her father seemed unloving at times and too harsh. She thought she would be better off here. Pavel seemed kind, and she liked Galina. She drifted off to sleep.

Raja awoke to the sound of the roosters. A large bowl of barley and two thick slices of cheese were set beside her. Cheese wasn't something she had eaten before. She tried it and liked the taste. She easily finished her meal.

The rest of the day was like a whirlwind. She first had lessons in how to pick up her food when eating, and how to use a linen napkin to wipe her chin. She was told to keep her hands and nails scrupulously clean, to not dip her meat directly into the saltcellar, and to always wipe her mouth before drinking. And with a great emphasis on its importance, she was taught how to curtsy in the presence of the lord and his lady.

Then Raja learned how to perform her duty as a scullery maid. She worked in the kitchen building inside the courtyard. She washed all the pots and bowls and any other dishes. She scrubbed the floor on her hands and knees. And while the other servants were eating at the servants' dining hall, she would stay in the kitchen to keep an eye on the food that was cooking.

At first, the servants were a bit distant toward Raja, as she was still seen as a field peasant. They held a sense of superiority over her, and occasionally, someone would be rude to her. But it didn't take long for them to change their attitude toward her. Raja never had an unkind word to say, and she promptly finished all her tasks with diligence. And any extra time was spent helping other servants with their own work.

The servants began to appreciate her and said that she had come at just the right time. The manor was expecting guests in the next while, and there was a lot to prepare until then. It was all hard work, but Raja was not going to complain. She was thankful to be there. And what was more, she was thankful for not having to get married.

However, Raja was most grateful for the late afternoons. She always felt exhausted by the end of the workday, but it wasn't the same kind of exhaustion she felt in the village and out on the fields. She had been here nearly four weeks now, and she certainly didn't miss the harsh work of being a peasant in the extreme heat or severe cold. She did think of her parents though. It was true her father had been harsh but not always, and nonetheless, she still loved him. Her mother was kinder. She missed both of them.

Pavel, as of late, had been going out of his way to spend time with her. For what reason, she didn't know. In the evenings, he began teaching her the alphabet and then concentrated on teaching her how to play chess. She caught on surprisingly well.

He had even given her a few rides on the back of his horse in the fields beyond the manor. She had never had so much fun before.

Raja focused her thoughts on the present again. She wondered about the guests everyone was talking about and whether there would be anyone her age. But she didn't think she would be allowed to play with them, seeing as how she was only a servant.

Galina entered Raja's room with the evening meal. Today's meal was deer meat, potatoes, gravy, and vegetables. This was a luxury for Raja.

"You are doing well," said Galina. "The lady of the manor is taking note of your hard work."

"Thank you," said Raja.

"The Odyhuns are coming this evening. But you must stay in here. You are not ready to serve other nobility."

Raja didn't understand who the Odyhuns were. She had no education at all. She did not even know how to read or write a single word.

"These guests, are they from a long way off?"

"Yes, they live east of Zurkia in the Odyhun Empire. Odyhun is the most eastern country in the Land of Rousse."

"How many countries are there?"

"Seven."

"How do you know that?"

"I learn a lot of things when I serve the nobility," said Galina, nodding with raised eyebrows.

"What do they want?"

"They're bringing a gift for the lord."

"What is the gift?" asked Raja with curiosity.

"I don't know. But I will have my ears open." Galina raised a finger to warn Raja. "Remember, don't stray from the room."

Raja nodded in agreement.

After their conversation, Galina left, and Raja watched for the guests out of the open window. Sometimes, when visitors came, it meant an exchange of peasants. At the age of four, she had arrived at this village in a cart. The cart only had room for her and her parents. They had first come from a different village that she couldn't remember much about. Her parents had been separated from their family from yet another village a long time ago. That's all they ever told her. They never talked of the reason why it happened. But they were always afraid it would happen again.

Raja heard the pounding of horses' hooves in the distance. The drawbridge was lowered. As the horses neared the castle, she counted six riders. They wore helmets with very long spikes. Black cloth covered part of their faces, causing her to feel uneasy with their unusual appearance. Their armor was green and black, and their shields, a bright orange. Raja noticed that one of the riders seemed considerably smaller than the rest and wore a niqab, which concealed the face. She wondered why a younger person would ride with a band of armored men. The scene was strange indeed. She had hoped to meet someone her age in amongst the guests, but these certainly weren't the guests she was expecting.

She heard scuffles and shouting outside as the servants rushed to accommodate the riders. The look of the armored guests made chills go up and down her body and she wished they would be sent away. But of course, her feelings made no difference, and under Viktor's consent they were let into the manor. After things quieted down Raja left the window to rest on her bed. She instantly fell asleep.

Chapter 3

Escape

A hand covered Raja's mouth. She woke up on her bed with a fright; she wanted to scream.

"Shhh, stay quiet. I'm here to help you. You are in danger, and we need to hide as quickly as possible."

A figure wearing a hooded niqab leaned over Raja, imploring her to be quiet. The intruder's hand relaxed over Raja's mouth. A feeling of bewilderment and confusion overwhelmed her.

"You must trust me. I will explain later," said the intruder.

The voice was quiet, but Raja could tell it was the voice of someone young. The moonlight through the window outlined the dark form. It was slender. Raja felt somewhat more at ease.

"Are you a girl?" Raja asked the figure, whose eyes were well hidden by the hood.

"Yes, we need to go quickly."

Remembering the veiled young rider with the armored men, Raja grew frightened by the thought of following her. Her suspicion of the girl held her back. It didn't make sense for her to leave the manor where she had been treated well.

"Why should I trust you?"

"Please," said the girl. "I'm here to help you. You do not know the urgency."

"You have no proof," said Raja.

Opposing thoughts battled inside Raja's mind. It was true the girl had no proof, but what if she was telling the truth? She quickly thought of something to say. "Leave my room or I shall scream!"

"No!" said the girl. "It will be the end of you. I have proof. Wait here."

The girl quickly stepped outside Raja's chambers and within moments came in with a woman. "This is my lady-in-waiting. She is looking out for me while I am here. The proof will be in her words."

"Raja," said the woman. "It is true. You are in danger and must leave the castle at once. But, Viktor is not the one to be feared, and Galina is a friend of mine. We share secrets."

"I've never met you before. How do I know you are Galina's friend?"

"Galina told me something about you."

Wondering what that possibly could have been, Raja waited for her answer.

"She told me that your name means hope."

Surprised by her statement, and then having a feeling deep down that they could be trusted, she relented and agreed to go with the girl. "I believe you, but why am I in danger?"

"There is no time to explain," said the girl. "We must leave the manor. Do you know how we can escape?"

The lady-in-waiting interrupted. "Galina told me that you know the secrets of the manor."

Raja nodded. "I do, but we will need warm clothing." She grabbed her satchel and put her candle and two of her shawls inside it. The girl quickly said a farewell to her lady-in-waiting and then turned to face Raja.

"Follow me," whispered Raja. It was true. Raja knew of every passageway in the manor. Working alongside Galina had given her an opportunity to learn everything about the architectural design and its camouflaged entrances. Galina had been entrusted with that knowledge and had passed on those secrets to Raja. She didn't know why Galina had entrusted her with that information but now she was glad of it.

They walked down a long corridor. They could hear shouts of laughter and loud singing coming from the great hall below. The guests were being entertained with much food and wine. They would be up late with their grandiose eating and merriment.

The girls finally came to a set of narrow stairs. They slowly made their way down the dark, winding stairs, pressing their hands against the cold wall for guidance. The stairs led into a small room. The room was empty, except for a small bed. Raja felt against the far wall, then stopped.

"Help me push against the wall," said Raja.

The two pushed with all their might, and the wall slowly rotated. They slipped inside the wall and closed off the entrance behind them. Walking sideways, they felt their way along the very narrow space and came to an open window. A thick, knotted rope was tied to one of the bars of the window. Raja lifted three of the bars that were cut near the bottom of the window and slid them upward into the wall. She pivoted a panel under the bars to prevent them from falling back down. There was plenty of space for them to go through the window.

"Help me tie my satchel to my head," said Raja. The girl did as Raja asked. "We must throw this rope over the window and climb down the side of the wall."

The two girls gathered the heavy rope and let it fall into the darkness below. It hung just above the water that surrounded the walls.

"Can you swim?" asked Raja.

"Yes," said the girl.

"Good. I'll go first. Hold yourself up on the knots if you need a rest."

The girl nodded. Raja climbed through the window and hung onto the rope. She rappelled herself down toward the murky moat. When she reached the end of the rope, Raja let her body splash into the water. The water was frigid. She struggled to keep afloat with her clothes weighing her down. The distance that she had to swim was not that far, and she made it to the other side of the moat, but she still felt quite out of breath.

Raja waved for the hooded girl to come. The girl slowly made her way down and plunged into the water. She struggled to come to the surface. Raja could see that she was having difficulty in the water. The girl was finding it more and more strenuous to keep afloat. Raja scanned the water's edge for anything that would help her.

Relief came as she spotted a large piece of an old log. "I'm coming," said Raja. "Don't panic!"

Raja splashed into the cold water again and, kicking with her legs, moved the log toward the girl. The girl grabbed it, and Raja helped her push the log to the edge of the moat. Raja pushed herself out of the water and then extended her arm to help the girl.

Exhausted and shivering, they ran down the Cabane Path that led into the woods. Thankfully, light from the moon made it possible for them to see. The path became narrower, and branches swiped against their bodies. Raja held up her hands to protect her face.

"Ahhh!" cried Raja as she tripped over a stone.

"Are you all right?" asked the girl.

"My ankle. It's hurt."

The girl knelt and felt Raja's ankle. "I don't think it's broken. Put your arm around my neck. I'll help you."

The two struggled down the path. Raja felt a throbbing pain in her ankle with every step. They could hear the night noises of the woods. A wolf howl pierced the quiet. Several more sounded. Chills ran up Raja's spine. Knowing timber wolves were dangerous, the sounds now frightened her. She remembered hearing wolf stories of men going out and never coming back.

"Are you afraid of wolves?" whispered Raja.

"Yes," said the girl. "Are you?"

"Very," said Raja.

"Are we almost there?"

"It's not much further," said Raja.

The desperation of the situation kept Raja moving. She exerted all of her energy to keep going, even though the throbbing pangs intensified.

"Stop," said Raja. "This is it."

Before them was a large tree. It had numerous short branches protruding from its trunk.

"We need to climb this tree."

The two girls ascended the tree. It was easy to climb, and in a short time, they were in the thick of the branches. Raja climbed onto a wooden structure supported by the branches, and the girl followed. The walls of the wooden structure prevented any light from coming in.

"This is the tree house of the lord's son. He used to play here when he was a boy. He showed it to me one day."

"What's his name?" asked the girl.

"Pavel."

"Is he kind?"

"Yes, very kind."

The girls sat across from each other. Darkness completely surrounded them.

"Are you okay?" asked the girl.

"Yes," said Raja. "How about you?"

"Fine, but cold."

"Do you want to put on a dry shawl?"

"Appreciated. My teeth are beginning to chatter."

Raja pulled out the shawls she had packed in her satchel. She gave one to the girl, and the other, she kept for herself.

"Here," she said. "Please put it over yourself."

The girls replaced their outer wet garments with dry shawls. The wool felt warm against their shivering bodies.

Raja took out the candle from her satchel. She fumbled around for two flint stones that were always kept in the tree house. She found them, along with a dry piece of moss. Raja repeatedly struck the stones together until smoke rose up from the moss. She blew air into the smoldering foliage. She had a flame.

Raja held the wick to the flame, and the candle was lit.

Light filled the small space.

Chapter 4

Deception or Truth

Raja held the candle up to the girl's face. She slowly lowered the candle in disbelief. "Who are you?" she asked.

"My name is Hannah Avaran."

"You look just like me. I feel like I must be dreaming!"

"Me, as well," said Hannah.

"Your red hair, your hazel eyes, and your skin color. They're all the same and even the shape of your nose. How can this be?" asked Raja.

"We are related."

"How? My parents are peasants in the village."

"Those are not your real parents."

Raja sat inside the tree house, stunned, and unable to believe what she was hearing.

"Look at me. Look at my hair, my face, and my eyes. You said so yourself. We are too much alike. You have to believe me," said Hannah.

"Tell me more."

"Your real name is not Raja. It is Chamaris."

"Chamaris?"

"Yes."

"Go on," said Raja.

"We are cousins. My father is Prince Narken, but he is called the Dark Prince. We live in Bolger Castle, which is north of Kazan."

Raja sat for a few seconds digesting that information. "You live in a castle?"

"I do, and a splendid one at that."

"Why is your father called the Dark Prince? That doesn't sound like a good name."

"He wants to overthrow the throne of Zurkia and does evil deeds to gain control of the country. I have seen much of his wickedness and lust for power."

Raja shuddered.

"And now, he is using me to accomplish his deeds," said Hannah.

"I can't imagine that."

"It's true."

"But why am I in danger?"

"You are next in line for the throne. And once they rid of you, the rest is easy for them."

Raja held up her hand to stop her. She sat silent for a while. She didn't want to believe it.

"What about my parents in the village? How did I get there?"

"When you were a very young child, Kazan Castle was raided, and you were abducted. But, they didn't want to kill you, so instead they put you with a peasant family, thinking you would never be discovered."

"So, my real parents are royal?" asked Raja.

Hannah nodded. "My father has always known where you were, but after he discovered that you were taken to the manor, he now has other plans to prevent you from ever inheriting the throne."

Breathing onto her hands to make them warm, Raja tried to dismiss from her mind what seemed very unreal to her. "You are frightening me. Why are you telling me all this?"

"I am here to warn you and protect you from the Odyhuns. They have come from the east and are conspiring with my father. The Odyhuns will offer a great price for you. They believe your lord will not turn it down."

Raja didn't have words to speak.

Hannah continued. "Then after you are gone, my father wants to use me as your imposter."

"He'll force you to do that?" asked Raja, thinking that Hannah's father must really believe he had control over her.

"He believes I am on his side."

Raja stared into Hannah's face, wanting to make sure that she was innocent of any wrong intent. "But is it really your father who wants the throne?"

Looking a bit frustrated, Hannah said, "Yes of course. I know that my father should not be the ruler of Zurkia."

Raja pulled the shawl tighter around her shoulders and held her hands to the warmth of the candle. Hannah did the same and continued speaking.

"I told my father that to be certain his plan would work, it would be a good idea to make sure that we truly look alike, as he believes, so I suggested that I ride here with the Odyhuns."

"You are ingenious."

Hannah smiled and tapped her head with her finger.

Raja smiled back, but she wondered how Hannah's father could have become so evil. "How did your father get this way?"

"Jealousy. He thinks he would be a better ruler than the tzarina."

Raja knew that jealousy brought about evil. "How did he come to be so jealous?"

"There are other influences in the family."

"Family?"

"Through marriage, but it's very complicated. Now is not the time to go into details."

Raja studied the girl who sat across from her. She didn't know Hannah, but she had apparently saved her life from tragedy. It seemed Hannah had put herself in a dangerous position on account of her own convictions. Raja saw that and admired her bravery. Her face was determined and serene. She wondered what Hannah saw in her. She was sure it was shock and fright.

"Thank you for saving me," said Raja.

"It is my duty and a statement of my faith."

"Will you stay here with me?"

"No, I have to go before they find out I have left the manor. But you must stay here for the night and return in the morning. It's not safe for you to go back until after the Odyhuns have left."

"All right, here, take my satchel. You can put your cloak and shawl in it when you cross the moat so they don't get wet."

Hannah graciously took the satchel. "Thank you. That's very kind of you."

Just before Hannah turned to go down the tree she turned to Raja and said, "Don't tell anyone of this conversation. Nobody must know about me, or my lady-in-waiting. And remember, whatever happens, we are friends forever."

"God keep you safe," said Raja. Hannah was just about to leave, but Raja wanted to ask her one more question. "Is the tzarina my mother?"

"Yes."

"So, she sits on the throne?"

"Yes." And with that last answer, Hannah disappeared into the dark.

Raja lay down on the wooden planks. She tried to think. If she stayed here until morning the Odyhuns could still search for her and find her here. And even if the Odyhuns left, Pavel and his father would find her here. The situation sounded scary to her. Maybe the lord would be tempted to accept the offer made by the Odyhuns.

Raja wasn't sure she wanted to go back to the manor. Right at this moment she felt very frightened to know someone wanted to buy her. And how did she even know Hannah's story was true? Perhaps lies had been told to Hannah, as well, and everything was a conspiracy, because they just wanted her for a different reason. Hannah's story about her father being the Dark Prince was hard to imagine. But if it was true, Raja certainly didn't want to be his target or anyone else's.

Raja's head was reeling. She was an heir to the throne? Her mother was the tzarina? That sounded absurd. There might be a Dark Prince, but she was not royalty. She was the daughter of her parents in the village. And right now, she missed them. She would go back to them and they would protect her. No one would find her there. Her parents would welcome her back, and she would work hard for them, so hard that they would not want to marry her off.

Raja carefully climbed down the tree with her ankle still throbbing. She thought about going down the Cabane Path again and taking the route along the tree line beside the fields. But it was a long walk and would probably take her over an hour. Instead, she decided to walk in the opposite direction towards the river. The river looped around the forest and came alongside the village. She thought the route would be shorter, and there would be less chance of anyone seeing her.

Raja hurried as fast as she could down the path towards the river, cringing with the pain she felt in her ankle. She had to keep going, before they found her. Branches got in her way, and she struggled to push them away. Relieved, she heard the river in the distance. It didn't take her much longer, and she was at the river's edge.

She began walking along the shore, but it soon became too steep and rocky to walk any further. She would have to turn back, but now doubted that she would even make it to the village with her injured ankle.

Raja whispered a prayer. Then, at the last second, before she turned back, something dark hidden amongst the rocks caught her attention. Could it be what she was hoping for? Her hopes proved right: a bundle of driftwood lay on the rocks with a paddle stuck in between the wood. The raft was a message in a bottle - she would survive.

Using the paddle, she managed to pry the raft upwards, and with not too much trouble she launched the raft into the river. It was a slow-moving river so she was safe. She slowly meandered down the river. The moonbeams bounced on the rippling water.

She heard the dipping of her paddle and the chirps of the crickets. A peace came over her as she passed through the arch of an overhanging tree. A serene feeling of protection encompassed her soul.

Raja finally reached the village. Moving closer to the shore she slipped off the raft and pushed it onto the rocks. The first hut of the village was just ahead. Her hut was the third one in the row of mud stone houses. A few more steps and she quietly slid past the curtain door.

She heard the clipping of her paddle and the chirps of the crickets. A peace came over her as she passed through the arch of an overhanging tree. A serene feeling of protection encompassed her soul.

Raja finally reached the village. Moving closer to the shore she slipped off the raft and pushed it onto the rocks. The first hut of the village was just ahead. Her hut was the third one in the row of mud stone houses. A few more steps and she quietly slid past the curtain door.

Chapter 5

Sword against Sword

The loud hollering and laughter continued far into the night. The guests followed no rules inside the hall of the manor. They chucked their gnawed bones all over the floor, they tossed their goblets in the fireplace during their drinking contests, and they wiped their grubby hands and faces on what was once the beautiful tablecloth. And when they blew on their soup to cool it off, it splattered everywhere.

The lord of the manor, Viktor Ramazon, was disgusted. On several occasions, he was tempted to ask his son to leave to spare him from seeing the crude behavior. He decided he needed to put an end to this.

Standing to make an announcement, Viktor caught everyone's attention. He was a good-looking man with thick, dark hair that fell to his shoulders. "Grand Padesha Tzoycha, you have come to pay us an anticipated visit. Now, please tell me what your intentions are for this visit."

The padesha stood up. He had taken off his helmet and replaced it with a coronet with colored jewels embedded around the outside of the headpiece. Baggy pants beneath a kaftan were exposed underneath his light armor. He began speaking. "A magnificent visit, indeed. Let us state our purpose in our coming. It is known by certain people that you have a beautiful, fair maiden that serves in your manor. It is said she is the most beautiful in all the Land of Rousse."

"Who are these 'certain people'?" asked Viktor.

"If I am not mistaken, it is the Dracians from the south that you have sold and traded goods with. I, too, have dealings with them."

"Fair enough, but all of my maidens are owned by this manor and none are at your disposal."

"I am speaking of the one with the red hair, and my offer is substantial."

"There is no such person here."

"Ah, but you may change your mind when you hear my offer. I speak of twenty-five thousand silver coins. She will be treated well and married to a crown prince in Dracon."

"Save your breath. I tell you, this person is not here."

"Come now, Lord Viktor. You could do a lot with twenty-five thousand coins. With that many coins, you could build another manor elsewhere, and your profits would be doubled."

"I already own two manors, and I do not need more. I am busy enough."

"I offer you double—fifty thousand coins."

Viktor abruptly stood and spoke in a commanding voice. "I tell you, there is no such person here. You are no longer welcome; I ask you to leave now!"

"We will not leave empty-handed! We demand a search!"

The group of Odyhun legionnaires took an offensive stance. The tension rose.

Viktor moved closer to the padesha and spoke to him in a low, stern voice. "You will have to fight me first with the sword."

"No. My son against yours," demanded the padesha.

The blood surged through Viktor. All eyes were on him, waiting for a reply. He grinned confidently.

"I consent."

The padesha's nostrils flared. He nodded in agreement.

Viktor immediately sent for his valet. Orders were given to take Pavel out of the room and ready him for the sword fight. Viktor himself was known to be the most skilled swordsman in Zurkia. He had taught his son everything he knew. Since the age of seven, his son had been practicing every day.

Pavel entered the room. He wore a light chain-mail vest with a sword tucked in his scabbard at the side. His opponent walked out in the open and stood opposite him, his own sword slung over his shoulder in a leather sheath. He, too, wore a thick vest for protection. Their hands were ready to draw their swords.

The padesha's loud voice cut through the silence. "Begin!"

The swords were drawn. Pavel gritted his teeth. With powerful blows, their swords locked together. They moved diagonally, forward, and backward. The Odyhun boy turned and struck. Pavel blocked the blow. With great speed, Pavel swished his sword in the air and struck again with more force, one after another in quick succession. He turned, and with both arms came down on the Odyhun's sword. The young Odyhun fell, and the tip of Pavel's blade was at his neck. It was over in a matter of seconds.

"Now for us!" shouted the padesha as he took off his coronet. He leaped out in front of Viktor.

"Very well," said Viktor. "Give me a sword!"

A sword hanging from the wall was quickly given to Viktor.

The padesha swished his sword viciously in the air. Viktor backed away, turned, and then struck. The padesha squatted, missing the blow. Standing again, the padesha repeatedly struck Viktor's sword with great force. Viktor returned the strikes and they both stepped backward and forward with precise movement of feet and clashing of steel.

The padesha turned and hurled himself to the other side of the table. He ripped the cloth off. The dishes smashed to the floor. He leaped onto the table. Viktor did the same with an acrobatic somersault. They advanced back and forth on the table.

Viktor stepped backward but immediately stepped forward again. He struck with a hard blow, turned and struck, and turned and struck. The padesha fell back onto the floor, and Viktor leaped down and had his sword to his neck.

"You have been defeated. Now leave. You have come here for purposes of which we do not believe in. Take your coin and go. Do not pay us another visit."

The padesha relented. "You have won. We will leave."

Viktor let go of his hold.

The padesha rose, brushed off his clothes, and put his coronet back on. He then ordered his men to leave. The men hastily made their way through the hall. The padesha walked past Viktor, but then, walking past Pavel, he unexpectedly grabbed Pavel from behind and put his dagger to his neck.

"We will search, or this boy dies!" shouted the padesha. He ordered his men. "Search the manor!"

The Odyhuns obeyed and marched through the building. They went into every room and searched every possible space. The servants were terrified and tried to stay out of their way.

The Odyhuns, with their swords drawn and ready to battle, returned to the hall with a young girl wearing a niqab.

"Who is that!" asked the padesha pointing to the girl.

"Hannah!" said the legionnaire.

Anger rose in the padesha's face. "Where is the girl we are looking for?"

"She is not here!" said the legionnaire.

The padesha was furious and shouted at Viktor. "This won't be the last!" He let go of Pavel and pushed him aside. "You can have your son back but you can't have the girl!"

"Leave!" shouted Viktor. "Now! Or there will be war!"

The padesha grunted and ordered his men to depart. The Odyhuns retrieved their horses and readied themselves to leave. The drawbridge was lowered with the chain. The Odyhuns mounted and galloped away with Hannah riding in their midst on her own white horse.

Viktor went around the manor to calm everyone and to see that no one was hurt. Pavel raced up to the maids' sleeping quarters. He knocked on Raja's door. There was silence. He knocked again, louder, but still no answer. He stepped in, but the room was empty. Her bed was slept in, but unmade.

Pavel returned to the hallway. The lady of the manor stood in the hallway looking at her son.

"Pavel, what's wrong?" she asked. Her eyes were dark but soft, and her hair was jet-black. She was elegantly poised and beautiful.

The lord came up behind his wife.

"Raja. She is not here," said Pavel with great concern.

"How is that possible?" asked the lord. "Do you think they misled us into believing she wasn't here and actually took her?"

"It's possible. Maybe the young girl with the niqab, whom we saw riding away, was really Raja."

"Perhaps, but the girl didn't act frightened in any way, so I don't think so. And besides, I am quite sure I saw that girl come in when the Odyhuns arrived."

"True," said Pavel.

"Let's hope we are right. We will look for her until we find her," said the lord.

Viktor ordered everyone to try and get some sleep. They would start to search at the first break of light.

Chapter 6

The Reunion

Raja's parents were asleep on a few bags of straw on the dirt floor of their hut. Their heads rested on two logs. They had one feather blanket. Guilt and love overcame Raja at the same time.

She walked by the goats and chickens nestled in the corner of the hut. She had nearly forgotten what it was like to sleep with the animals. She ran her hand along the crude trestle table. She didn't want to wake her parents. They needed their sleep. She wondered again whether she was doing the right thing. She would be a village peasant again. That life would be hard. She lay down on top of the table. For now, at least, she had the warmth of the embers from the fire. She soon drifted off to sleep.

Yana woke up and it didn't take her long to notice that someone was on the table. She quickly nudged her husband.

"Antom, there's someone sleeping on our table," she whispered.

"What did you say? Don't talk nonsense. It's only the goat that escaped." Antom mumbled some more and turned over.

"It is not a goat. It's a girl."

"Well, get up and see for yourself then. But don't bother me."

Yana warily walked over to the table and looked at the girl's face. "Pray that it may be. It's Raja!" said Yana.

"Who?"

"Raja."

"Well, give the girl something to eat then," Antom said calmly as if he'd been expecting her all along.

Raja opened her eyes and looked into her mother's face. She immediately sat up and hugged her mother.

"Raja, you are here. I have not stopped crying. Let me look at you. You are beautiful." Yana put her hands over her face and cried.

Antom got up from bed and put a hand on Raja's shoulder. "I am glad you have come home."

"I have missed you both," said Raja.

"Sit down, and we will have breakfast. You must tell us what happened," said Antom.

Antom put wood on the smoldering embers that lay in a pit surrounded by rocks in the middle of the room. A pot hung over the burning fire, and Yana stirred the pottage. Raja got up to open the shutters on the window so the smoke could escape. The pottage was served with goat's milk and black bread. They ate it gratefully. Raja began to recount her story.

"They were kind to me. The work was good. But something terrible has happened. There were Odyhuns that came. And there was this girl. She said she was my cousin, and she looked just like me. But she said I was royalty, and someone wanted me."

Raja's parents seemed uncomfortable with the story. They were silent, but Antom motioned for her to continue as he sat on a trunk, carving an image in a piece of wood.

"The girl said her father was the Dark Prince, and he wanted the throne. And the Odyhuns were trying to buy me. So I was afraid and didn't want to go back to the manor. I thought I would be safe here." Raja took a spoonful of her pottage. It was hot so she blew on it and then continued speaking. "I don't know if I believe what the girl said to me. You are my parents, and I know you will protect me from those people."

Yana and Antom seemed nervous and were very quiet. Then Raja remembered that she had promised to keep the conversation secret. Why hadn't she? She blamed it on her fear. She decided to say no more. "Please don't tell anyone that I told you this."

"You have our promise. We will do everything to protect you," said Antom. "And I am also asking you not to tell anyone else this story."

Raja agreed.

"But listen. You cannot stay here. This is the first place they will look for you. I will talk to our friends about it," said Antom.

Arrangements were made with the Eyem family three huts down. They, of course, remembered Raja and welcomed her into their meager, small home. The dwelling had a few more amenities than Raja's hut. The dirt floor was covered in straw to provide warmth, and pallets were slept on at night. The mother and father were reserved, and both had worn faces from the sun. Raja had worked with their two children, the girl being one year younger and the boy two years younger. She felt glad to be in their company.

Raja went to work immediately. She collected eggs from the chickens and would make sure to shut them in their cages at night. Then she got vegetables from the garden and prepared a thick pottage for the evening meal. While it was still light out, she was given a few clothes to mend. The mother of the hut was busy weaving wool that she had earlier sheared from a few sheep. The father had spent the day in the field harvesting and storing wheat from the lord's fields. Both the woven wool and the wheat were given to the lord.

Darkness for the peasants always came as a relief. It meant the day was finished, and rest and sleep were permitted. The parents of the Eyem family generously gave up their sleeping pallet to Raja and their two children, while they themselves took the children's pallets and slept in the main room.

Raja and the two children put on warm clothing and stretched out on the straw mattress. The children were curious about Raja and began to ask her questions.

"Where did you go?" asked the girl whose name was Xenia.

"I was working for the lord in his manor."

"Did you like it?"

"It was much better than working in the fields."

"Why did you come back?"

"That is something I can't tell you."

Xenia looked at Raja with sincerity in her eyes. "You can trust me. I won't tell anyone. I can keep a secret."

Raja had missed the companionship of people her own age. She felt very tempted to tell them, and she did trust them. "Okay, but you must not tell anyone." The children earnestly nodded. "A girl, who is supposed to be my cousin told me that I am royalty and that it was unsafe for me at the manor."

The two children were wide-eyed.

"Do you mean you are a princess?" asked Xenia.

"Hush," said Raja. "Yes."

"Just like in the tales?"

"I guess so, but I don't think it's true. I don't see how it could be."

"Well, let's just pretend then."

The three children giggled.

"Okay, I'll be the princess," said Raja.

"Then I'll be another princess," said Xenia.

"And I'll be a knight," said Boris.

Raja thought the game was fun, and the three of them made up stories of knights and princesses. They eventually drifted off to sleep.

Morning came quickly. Raja and the children started their morning chores by taking the goats and sheep out to pasture. They then went to the fields of brush to pick berries and herbs. They made their work fun by acting out the stories they told to each other. They later came home to weed and harvest the garden. The work was never finished, and the days turned to weeks and the weeks to months. Raja wondered if Pavel had looked for her. No one had heard anything so she didn't think so. After all she was just a peasant.

Eventually Raja moved back into her own home. Her mother and father were glad and also relieved to have her again. Raja's mother was not that well a lot of the time, so Raja's help was very welcomed.

Talk was going around about the bonfire that was traditionally made to celebrate the end of the harvest. Usually, the wrestling, dancing, and singing would go on late into the night. Someone would also tell stories to make everyone wiser.

"Xenia, will you sit beside me at the bonfire tonight?" asked Raja.

"Of course," said Xenia.

Night came, and the girls made their way to the bonfire. Raja, still feeling uneasy about her past experience, pulled her hood closer to her face. The girls sat near the back of the crowd. The fire rose to enormous heights, and the festivity began.

Chapter 7

The Dream

The singing was boisterous and merry around the bonfire. The dancing was vigorous with twirls and spins. At the end of every dance, the men finished with a difficult acrobatic stunt. Their favorite stunt was squatting while folding their arms and kicking out their legs. The main beverage for everyone was ale, which seemed to add to the lively merriment.

Children started to gather around one particular man. He was the village's storyteller. He was older, and his face was weathered from the sun. He had a scar on the side of his face, but despite that, he still had a friendly look.

"Tonight," he said, "I have a very intriguing story and a gift for the best interpretation of the story."

"A gift?" asked the children in unison.

"Yes, a gift you will all like," said the storyteller.

"Please choose me," said some of the children.

"I can only choose one, so listen carefully."

Raja listened as the story was told.

Angelica's Beautiful Feather

There once was a girl, whose name was Angelica, who lived in a small village. She had two wonderful talents, which were being generous and molding clay pots. People came from all over the country to look at her pots and gave her coin in exchange for her work. Merchants would marvel at her talent and beg her to work for them. But she told them that she did not want to work for anyone. All she wanted to do was stay in her village and use her coin to help other people.

One day, Tatchamee, the evil witch, heard of Angelica's beautiful work. She transformed herself into an old woman so she could pay the girl a visit. When she saw her talent for molding clay pots, she began to covet Angelica's fine work and wanted it for herself. Tatchamee tried to tempt the girl to come with her, by offering to make her princess of her kingdom. The witch told Angelica that she could have anything she wanted. But secretly, the witch wanted to turn the girl into her slave. Angelica refused her request by saying she would never leave her village. She loved her friends and family too much.

Her refusal made Tatchamee very angry, so she turned Angelica into a firebird. The witch then turned herself into a huge falcon and picked up Angelica in her talons. She flew toward the sea where she had her kingdom.

Angelica wanted to leave a piece of her love for her family and friends as a way of saying farewell. So, she plucked out her feathers and dropped them to the village below. She had but one feather left, which was the longest and most beautiful one. She was tempted to keep it, so she might die with her feather, but then, as she was carried over the last part of the village, she decided to pull out the feather and let it float to the villagers below as a gift to all.

Angelica felt weak and thought she would die. But, when the last feather reached the village, the falcon's talons opened, and she was released. All the other feathers swept upward and were part of her body again. The falcon flew off and always stayed a falcon, and from that day on she could never close her talons again and always soars in the sky with no rest.

The firebird flew back to the village and back to her home. When she got inside her house, she plucked out her most beautiful feather. She let it float down inside one of her clay pots. As soon as the feather floated inside the pot, the firebird turned back into Angelica and she was more beautiful than ever before. She blessed everyone who came to her, and grew in favor with the people. She keeps her feather to remind her of how beauty grows with goodness.

"Now," said the storyteller. "Before I ask for an interpretation, I have a gift for everyone."

"What is it?" asked the children.

"Honeycomb. It is very sweet, and you will like it." The children took the honeycomb and talked with excitement as they tasted the sweet nectar. "Now, who can tell me the lesson of the story?"

The children were quiet and waited for someone to speak. They continued sucking on their honeycomb. Some children poked their sticks in the fire and watched the ends of their sticks burn. Xenia and Boris, too, played with the fire. Nobody seemed to have an answer for the storyteller.

Finally, Raja offered her thoughtful explanation.

"Angelica thought it was better to serve the ones around her with love rather than please the greediness of other merchants. Angelica was nearly defeated by evil, but her selfless actions saved her, and she was restored with greater blessings than before."

"Bravo," said the storyteller. "Very good. I didn't know we had such a bright one among us. And what is the moral of the story?"

Raja thought for a moment.

"Beautiful things happen to those who do good."

"Well, now. You are the wise one. I have not heard it said so well."

The people in the crowd clapped. Raja stood up and took a bow. The people laughed. Then they stood up and took a bow. Everyone laughed some more, and the dancing and singing started all over again. More ale was poured, and the night's festivities continued.

The storyteller handed out more pieces of honeycomb to the children. They thankfully took it and savored it in their mouths.

Giving another piece of honeycomb to Raja, the storyteller sat beside her. "Here is the gift that I promised."

He gave Raja a little doll about the size of her hand.

Raja gasped. "For me? I love it. How did you get this? I have never seen anything so pretty."

"The tzarina gave this doll to the young lord and now he has asked me to give it to you."

"The young lord knows I am here?"

"Yes, he knows. But he is glad you are safe and happy. He doesn't want to force you to go back to the manor if you don't want to."

"And you say the tzarina gave it to the young lord?"

"Yes."

"Do you think she wanted the lord to give it to me?"

"It sounds reasonable."

"I see," said Raja.

The storyteller looked into Raja's eyes. "But it is not only on account of the tzarina that you have this gift. I have a feeling the young lord misses you, because he asked about you when I was in the manor telling one of my stories."

Raja lowered her eyes. "I am just a peasant. Why would he be interested in me? We are much too different."

"Perhaps, but perhaps not. May I see the doll?"

Raja gave the storyteller the doll.

"How many fingers does the doll have?"

"Ten."

"How many fingers and toes?"

"Twenty."

"Good, you remembered. Well then, how many pearls does this doll have?"

The storyteller watched carefully as Raja counted the pearls.

"Twenty-four."

"I'm surprised. You will do well."

The storyteller gave the doll back to Raja. She studied it some more. She loved the design of the embedded white pearls and silky lace. She was thankful for the gift but wondered why Pavel had given it to her. She thought she didn't deserve it and didn't think she would ever see Pavel again.

She again looked at the storyteller and held the doll to his chest. "Perhaps you should give the doll back. I don't think I will ever go to the manor again."

The storyteller pushed the doll back towards Raja. "No. Pavel said that you must keep it. And it's not good to disobey orders."

Raja looked at the doll again and then tucked it under her sash. "Where did you learn that story?"

"I learned it in a southern country while I was a merchant sailor. I also learned other languages and stories, and I became known as a storyteller."

"How did you come to this village?"

"It's a long story."

"Tell me," said Raja with curiosity.

"I was sold into slavery."

Raja's eyes grew wide. "How did that happen?"

With a bit of sadness in his eyes, the storyteller continued to tell his story. "I used to be a merchant sailor. One day, sea pirates invaded my ship." The storyteller pointed to his face. "Do you see my scar? They did that to me, and they also took my daughter."

"What happened to her?"

"I don't know."

Raja could see the pain in the storyteller's face. "I'm sorry to hear that."

"I appreciate your care," said the storyteller.

"Please tell me what happened next."

"The pirates sold me into slavery, and I was taken into the northern region of Zurkia. After some time, I was sold to the Odyhuns, but before they could take me away, someone intervened and offered to buy me again at a greater price."

"And so now you are here?"

"I am."

"Was it the lord who bought you?"

"Yes, and he has treated me well. I go to the manor and entertain guests with my stories. I think that is the reason he bought me. He loves to hear the stories."

"I love them too," said Raja. "Could you tell me another story?"

"I would be pleased to."

"Tomorrow?" asked Raja.

"Tomorrow," said the storyteller.

The storyteller was about to get up and leave when he decided to say something more. "There has been something on my mind."

"What is it?" asked Raja feeling very inquisitive.

"I'm not expecting you to discern what I want to say. However, it feels good just to talk about it with someone. But granted, you have already proven to be discerning."

Raja felt honored that he would choose to trust her with his matters of concern.

"I had a dream, but I'm not sure what it means," said Kuzma.

"I'd like to hear it," said Raja.

Kuzma looked into Raja's eyes with a serious gaze and told her his dream.

It was an image of a glowing, bluish-white sphere. It descended from the heavens and settled in the sky just above me. But it grew smaller and smaller until it disappeared. I walked in a circle, looking for it in the sky, but then I tripped on a black box.

When I got up again, the box disappeared, and the sphere was before me, but this time no larger than a pea. It began to grow in size and was bigger and brighter than before. Then a crown appeared on top of the sphere.

"A very unusual dream," said Raja.

"How would you interpret it?" asked the storyteller.

"I think the large sphere represents something powerful happening in the future, but its disappearance represents tragedy."

Surprised at her intuitive answer the storyteller said, "Yes, a good interpretation. Do you see anything else?"

"The crown represents royalty."

Again, the storyteller was surprised at her answer. "I think you're right."

The storyteller's face grew serious and he was not quite ready to talk. Then, after a minute, he continued. "There's more. Do you know what a monk is?"

"Yes, it is a person dedicated to praying to God."

"Well, I had a monk visit me. He knew that I had this dream. He said that I must convey my dream to this certain person."

"Who is the person?" asked Raja.

"I don't know, but the monk had a vision of this person, and he described him to me. He lives in Demarcus Castle, just across the river to the south."

"I guess the best thing to do would be to go and visit him. I'm sure the lord would let you go."

"Hopefully," said the storyteller.

"I'm sure of it," said Raja.

The storyteller stood up.

"Don't forget our story time," said Raja.

Bowing, the storyteller said, "I won't."

The storyteller then went to watch the wrestling match that was about to begin. Raja couldn't wait until tomorrow to hear another story.

She looked at the commotion that was going on around the fire. There was a lot of fuss to do with betting on the contestants for the match. Everyone was fervently focused on the competitors, everyone except Raja. On the other side of the fire, she noticed an odd person—someone who sat alone and did not reveal his or her face. She thought perhaps it was a visiting peasant, as was sometimes the case.

The person got up and started walking around the fire and then walked toward her. A veil covered the person's face. It frightened her. Now, the person took quicker steps and came and stood right before her.

"Raja, it's me, Hannah."

Chapter 8

Gift of Silk

Raja was astonished that Hannah was standing right before her. "What are you doing here?"

"I have something very important to give you. But let's go where no one can see us."

Raja questioned Hannah a little further before she made up her mind to leave the bonfire. "How did you get here?"

"I came with the young bailiff of your manor. He is dealing with the accounts of the manor for your lord. My father doesn't suspect me and thinks that I am elsewhere."

"How do you know the bailiff?"

"Your lord's bailiff has connections with my lady-in-waiting. She arranged the ride for me."

"Okay," said Raja a little reluctantly. "Follow me."

While the wrestling was going on, the two girls slipped out and found their way into Raja's hut.

"Hannah," said Raja. "I don't know why you came to the manor, but I felt very frightened on that night. I am here now with my parents. We love each other, and I want to stay here."

"Raja, you are at the age where you could marry, and someone may want you again in this village or in another one. You can't let that happen."

"Surely it won't happen for a while," said Raja.

"Perhaps, but there are pressures. You must listen to me. I know you doubt what I say, but everything I have told you is true."

"You say that, but it is hard for me to believe the things that you told me," said Raja.

Hannah leaned closer toward Raja, and seriousness came over her face. "I have come to give you a gift. I think this may convince you that what I have said is true."

Hannah pulled out a package from inside her cloak. It was wrapped in beautiful silk material of all colors. She handed it to Raja.

"Oh!" she said. "It's lovely."

"Open it," said Hannah.

Raja carefully untied the string. She unfolded the material, and there lay a woven silk scarf of impeccable artistic design and striking color.

Raja ran her hand along the shiny scarf and the finely tasseled edge. The silk felt divinely smooth, just like the brushed hair on a horse's neck. Picking it up, she let it unravel. She studied the handiwork up close.

"Something is odd about this," she said. "I feel like I have seen this before."

A picture flashed in her mind. It was a memory. She was watching a woman weave this very scarf. The fabric, the color, the design—it all came back to her.

"This scarf, Hannah, I know this scarf. I remember it. This exact one."

Another memory flashed into Raja's mind.

"People in armor came. They burst into the room. Everyone was screaming."

"Can you remember more?" asked Hannah.

"Someone took the woman, and then someone grabbed me out of her arms. They ran with me down the hall, and then a different woman took me."

"What happened next?"

"I don't know. It's hard. I just remember being passed to more strange people." Raja was near to tears. "Why haven't I remembered this before?"

"Because you were very young, and this scarf helped to bring back this memory. This scarf is something that you could see with your eyes and feel with your fingers when you were a child. It was something that belonged to you."

Raja started to cry. "It is all so confusing. How could they do that? How could they rip me from my mother?" Looking at Hannah with anger, she yelled. "It can't be! No, it can't be!"

Hannah put a hand to Raja's face. "Hush Raja. I know this is difficult, but you must know the truth."

"Why did they do that? They stole me from my mother!"

Hannah's eyes were soft. "There is evil in this world, but no matter what, we must do our best to bring good."

"Do our best to bring good? After what happened?"

"Yes. It will only weaken you to stay angry."

Raja wiped the tears from her eyes and looked at the scarf. Then, after a moment said, "Yes, you are right. It will do no good for me to stay angry."

"You will only torment yourself. You must heal your soul."

"But how can I heal my soul if I'm here in this forsaken village?"

"Doing good will heal your soul. And that can happen in any circumstance."

"I agree, but how will that help elsewhere?"

"Goodness is like a wave on the sea. It starts out as a ripple and grows to something much greater."

Raja looked into Hannah's eyes, wanting to believe her. Somehow inside of herself, Raja knew Hannah was right, even though she believed her efforts would never leave her own little village. But by doing good, she could replace the anger she felt with joy.

"Raja, there's also a letter for you, and you must know what it says. The bailiff has asked me to give it to you. It was passed on to him by my lady-in-waiting."

Hannah took a folded, sealed letter from inside her boot. She carefully unfolded the letter and read it to Raja.

To Chamaris,

This is my silk scarf that I was weaving for you when you were a child. After you were taken, I could not find you anywhere. Your father also disappeared at the same time, but we do not know precisely what happened. However, by evidence, he is believed to have been in an accident and died. In my great grief, I continued to weave the scarf. And each time I worked on the scarf, I would pray that I would see you again. Please be it that you remember this gift so that I know everything is true.

Someone very trustworthy informed me that you were found in the village, and were taken to the manor. I believe that I am your real mother, but I know that your peasant mother and father are the ones who brought you up, and I understand the love that you would have for each other. But, if you are my daughter, I am imploring you to return to the manor. You may be given freedom to visit your parents. Your royal blood must not be thrown aside, and you must carry out your duty as heir to the throne of Zurkia. The manor nobility will teach you things you need to know in order to prepare you for this.

I have written another letter to the lord of the manor explaining the situation. If it is true that you are my daughter, then urge the bailiff to give it to the lord so he too will believe in your nobility. Instructions to all will be given for your care at the manor. Do not be afraid. I will command that guards be added to the estate for your protection. I wish you well, and do not be upset. Please accept that this is your predestined role in life.

Sincerely with love and in all hope,
Tzarina Valentina, who sits on the throne of Zurkia

Raja did not know what to say.

"Please accept it, Raja. Do you accept it?"

Raja looked at the scarf. She did remember the shiny silk material. It truly had belonged to the tzarina, who had been her mother. Even now, she could hear her mother sing as she wove the scarf. Raja ran her fingers over the soft colorful scarf in the same way she had when she was a child. Raja searched Hannah's eyes, wanting to believe that everything was true. Then a joyous smile came over Raja's face. Tears came to her eyes—yes, she did believe.

"I accept it," whispered Raja.

"Very well, Your Highness," said Hannah, who had tears of joy running down her cheeks.

"And very well to you, Your Excellency."

Raja wiped Hannah's tears from her face. The girls looked into each other's faces and giggled.

"Is this really true? It feels like a dream to me," said Raja.

Hannah took her cousin's hands and squeezed them. "It's not a dream. It is really true."

"My life has changed again. I wish you could stay here with me."

"That is not possible. But I'm sure we will see each other again."

"Yes, I will hope for it so we can be like sisters," said Raja in earnest.

"I hope for it too," said Hannah. "I am sure it will come to pass. I will tell the bailiff that you have decided to return to the manor. Pavel will be here tomorrow morning to bring you back to the estate."

Raja put her hand to her mouth and gasped in surprise. It seemed so surreal. Hannah gave Raja a knowing smile. The girls hugged each other, and Hannah disappeared again through the opening of the door.

Chapter 9

The Finishing Touch

Raja's mother and father thought Raja was doing the right thing. They would miss her greatly but it was best to do as the tzarina wished. Raja's parents now confessed that Raja had been given to them when she was three years of age, but they were forbidden to say anything about it to anyone. So, for all these years, it had been a secret.

They had not known Raja was royalty, so when they heard Raja tell them why she had escaped from the manor, it had worried her parents terribly. They became fearful and did not know whether to believe her story, but now they could see that it was true.

As Raja and her parents looked through the hut window, Pavel appeared with his horse in the distance. His image was regal. The pounding of the horse's hooves reached Raja's ears. She loved that sound.

"Whoa, boy," said Pavel as he slowed his horse to a trot. He came riding up alongside the hut. Raja was waiting for him. She hugged her parents and assured them she would be back to visit. Her father helped her get up on the back of the horse, but this time with pride.

"Hang on tightly," said Pavel.

Rearing his horse, Pavel then thundered up the hill to the manor. The horse's dark chestnut body glistened in the sun with its white mane and long tail catching in the wind. With her arms wrapped around Pavel's waist, Raja let the weight of her body rock with the horse's movement. The rhythm exhilarated her.

Raja glanced back at her parents. They were what she left behind, and the peasant way of life. There was nothing else. She only had two things now: her doll and her scarf.

In a matter of minutes, they arrived at the manor. Three bells sounded their arrival. Pavel helped Raja off the horse, and the maidservants escorted her away. This time, they took her to another part of the manor. The lady of the manor was waiting for her. She smiled affectionately at Raja.

"Welcome to our home, Raja. I hope you will find it most comfortable. If there is anything that you desire, please ask."

The lady of the manor curtsied, and Raja curtsied back and then continued to comply with the maid's directions. They guided her into a large room with a canopy bed and beautiful clothes, which were laid out across the bed. Beautifying her, the maids put her in a dress that Raja thought too elegant to touch.

"This dress was sent to you by your tzarina mother," said Galina. "She has certainly picked the right color of green for you."

"It's beautiful," said Raja.

The maids fussed over her hair and combed out her long tresses. They twisted it and covered it in fancy decorations.

"Wait," said Raja. "Please take out the decorations and put my scarf in my hair instead. It is on the bed."

"As you wish," said Galina. "I was worried you would never come back. But what an entrance you've made."

Raja smiled innocently. "I can't believe it myself. I think I shall have a lot of learning to do. How does one become a princess?"

"You will have a fine teacher in the lady of the manor," said Galina. "And just as importantly, I think you should be yourself."

Galina wove the scarf through Raja's hair at the back of her neck and tied it in a stylish knot. The colors and patterns were striking and made Raja look serene.

"The scarf gives me a wonderful feeling," said Raja. "I feel like I carry a small part of my tzarina mother when I wear it."

"I think the same way," said Galina. "It looks lovely on you. I have another surprise for you."

"What is it?"

"It is a gift from your tzarina mother."

Galina gave Raja a little wooden box. Raja opened the lid and picked up what she thought was the most exquisite piece of jewelry ever.

"Your mother sent you one of her crown jewels," said Galina.

Raja turned it over in her hands. It was a round, green emerald stone encircled by blue sapphires and embedded in gold. It hung from a gold link chain and sparkled each way Raja turned it. She counted the stones.

"Well now, who taught you how to count?" asked Galina.

"The storyteller. He said it would prove to be worthwhile for me someday."

"I don't doubt it will. Even I need to count when I cook."

Raja held the stone up against her dress. The colors were just right. She was in awe that she could ever own something like this. But it was precious to her because it had belonged to her mother. She silently thanked her for the gift.

Galina took the piece of jewelry and used it for the finishing touch of Raja's attire. She positioned the stone perfectly in the center of her forehead. She had a feeling the piece of jewelry would make Raja look like royalty. And she was right—when everything was in its perfect place, Raja looked like a princess.

It was time to join the upper-class for the evening meal.

Chapter 10

Three Requests

When Raja arrived at the hall entrance, Viktor's family, consisting of three members, were already seated. Servants were standing to the side of the table ready to serve when requested. As she entered the room, the family stood up from their seats and everyone in the room cheered.

"Your Highness!"

"Welcome, and please have a seat with us," said Viktor. "We are pleased that you have now made our home your home. The news has come to us that you are an heir to the throne—I stand corrected. You are the next heir to the throne."

The lord and his family bowed to Raja, and then sat in their seats, as did Raja, who took a seat beside Maya. Lord Viktor continued talking.

"We will do everything in our power to protect you and make you most comfortable. If you shall so desire anything, please make your wishes known. But you must remember, you are still very young, and training and discipline will still be in my power."

"Yes, my lord," said Raja.

Viktor bowed and then retrieved a sheet of parchment from his vest.

He continued. "I have here a short letter from your tzarina mother that must be read aloud at our first dining together now that you have returned. And then later, I shall read it again at the second and third dinner sitting with the guards and servants, at which time you will be introduced as the daughter of the tzarina."

Viktor carefully unrolled the scroll and read the letter.

To the most hospitable and gracious family of Lord Ramazon, who have always been my loyal and trustworthy servants,

Thank you for finding my lost daughter and for bringing her into your home. I beseech you to care for her and protect her with all diligence. She must not come to Kazan Castle, as it may not be safe. I have not been in contact with my brother, who as you are aware, has always claimed ownership of the throne, but I have received messages from certain sympathetic ears in his castle that he is, as of now, pursuing the throne in a more aggressive way. I feel that it is best for Raja's safety to stay where she is. And in the meantime, she must learn the way of the royals so she can come before me in a proper manner.

In further requests, please see to it that she is taught everything she needs to know for her future royal duties. Educate her well in every way. Pay special attention to music, languages, and history. And do not neglect mathematics, as this is the foundation of all knowledge. I feel confident that you, Chamaris, will do your best in all of these matters. Please adhere to the instruction of learning in the proper manner. I have full confidence that you will be treated well. I look forward to seeing you in the future and will send for you when the time is right.

Sincerely and with good intentions always,
The Tzarina Valentina

Lord Viktor looked at Maya and Pavel. Their faces were solemn. "The findings about the Dark Prince are troubling, but do not worry. The royalty, which now sits here with us, and the royalty of Kazan Castle, will be protected."

Pavel stood up. "Hear, hear Father. It will be as you say!"

Viktor nodded and he and his son sat down. The lord then waved his hand to the servants. "Please bring in the food that we may eat."

The servants brought in bowl after bowl. It was really too much for Raja, but she tried to eat as well as she could. The tastes were different, but also delicious.

Light conversation circled between the four members, and finally, near the end of the meal, the lord addressed Raja.

"Raja, is there anything at this time that you would like?"

Raja had listened intently to the letter and was waiting to see if an opportunity for a request was presented.

"Yes, my lord, there is," said Raja.

"Go on," said the lord.

"I request that my parents, Yana and Antom Domina, come live with us at the manor. They are good people and will work hard for you. Yana is a good baker, and Antom is a craftsman."

"Well now, I think we could use some more bakers. And I have already been enjoying Antom's craftsmanship, so it is as you request. Arrangements will be quickly made, and they will be given everything they need."

Raja was relieved. She felt joyful that she could live close to her parents and that they would not have to suffer the harsh life of being village peasants.

"Is there anything else, my princess?" asked the lord.

"Yes, there is," said Raja. "I would also like my parents' friends, who are also my friends, to come live with us. They, too, are good people and will serve you well. Their children are obedient, and they will be profitable for you."

The lord found the request quite bold and tried hard not to smile. Trying to retain a serious expression, he complied. "Well, I wasn't expecting two families, but I could use another blacksmith. Your wish is my command. They, too, will have everything that they need."

The family clapped. The lord motioned his hand to speak again, but Raja spoke first.

"My lord," said Raja.

"Yes, Your Highness."

"I do have another request."

"Certainly."

"The storyteller too?"

The lord's smile could not be held back. "Of course, Your Highness."

Pavel sat back with his arms crossed and observed the conversation with great amusement. He thought this was definitely the time for a toast.

He stood up holding his goblet and said, "May I present a toast for our new member of the manor. Long live the princess!"

The family responded in unison, "Long live the princess!"

Pavel continued. "Whom, I might add, is off to a very victorious start in her royal duties as princess."

Everyone cheerfully chuckled, and before Pavel sat down, Raja was sure she saw a twinkle in his eye. Her life was completely transformed again, and she was going to love sharing her new home with her parents and friends. What a dream come true it would be for them. But she wouldn't forget the villagers. She would make it her duty to visit and show as much kindness to them as she could.

Reflecting on the things her cousin had told her and what her new life would hold in the future, she wondered about her tzarina mother and what she looked like. Perhaps she was beautiful. Perhaps she had red hair and hazel eyes too.

Raja looked down at her doll. She thought it looked like herself. Feeling it had been a sign that she would be back at the manor, Raja clasped her doll in her hands, hoping to meet her mother one day in the future.

Part 2

Sword and Shield

Chapter 11

Victory is Mine

"I will win your battle. It is I who will defeat the enemy!" shouted Pavel as he thrust his lance upward and rode his horse around the outskirts of the playing field. "Victory is mine! I will show my strength!"

Crowds of spectators from neighboring manors and castles sat on benches alongside the playing field, which was not too far from Viktor's manor. Eager to watch the tournament, they shouted in response to the contestant's war cries.

"Forward! Raise your flags! Raise your power!"

"Victory!" shouted the squires as they passed each other on their horses. "Today is the day that will be your defeat! Fear in your lowly state!"

The squires continued to shout their war cries as they paraded alongside the spectators. Every horse was draped in cloth of a different color with elaborate designs and crests. Every squire was dressed in heavy armor and was determined to show his ability and skill. Their smooth helmets were made of thick metal, having no spikes to reduce the weight of the helmet.

A short blow of a bugle was heard. The opposing teams lined up on opposite ends of the field, made up of newly pronounced squires. Each held his lance close to his body. Their minds were focused. There was only one thing to think about: hit the opposing rider as hard and as accurately as possible.

Pavel's breathing came long and hard as his heart pounded. His horse pawed the ground with flared nostrils. A long blow of the bugle sounded.

"Urra!" shouted Pavel.

All the jousters shouted their war cries.

The spectators stood and shouted, "Onward, onward, show us your courage!"

The teams galloped their horses toward one another. Pavel focused and aimed. And at that very second, his lance struck with great force on the shield of his opponent. Pavel felt a sharp pain in his shoulder. The rider fell. Screams erupted from the spectators. A short blow of a bugle sounded, and the teams lined up once more. Pavel's team was down one, and the opposition was down two.

The riders continued another round. Pavel was struck hard in the chest and he fell to the side of his horse's neck, saving him from defeat. He ached from the blow, but adrenaline still raced through his body. There were three riders down on each team, and only three players remained on each side.

Pavel focused on the player opposite him. Blue and white were his opponent's colors. His thoughts raced through his mind as he peered through the slit in his helmet. "Don't take your eyes off that color. Not for a second. Bend forward and hold your lance close to your body for balance. Breathe steadily."

Again, the long blow of the bugle sounded above the roars of the crowd. The team players galloped forward, and in five seconds it was over. Pavel made it to the other side still on his horse. However, this time he was the only player left on his team, with two remaining on the other team.

The odds of Pavel winning were very slight. The signal was given, and he charged for the center of the two approaching horses. In the last few seconds, he cut in front and rode diagonally. Catching one of the riders off guard, Pavel aimed and thrust with all his strength. The rider was knocked off his horse, and he fell to the ground. Cheers rose from the crowd.

The playing field was even with Pavel's colors of red and white against blue and white. Pavel and his opponent took off their helmets and rode around the field alongside the spectators. In the middle of the spectators was a small covered area. In that area sat Raja, Pavel's mother, Galina, and a few other women. Pavel thought Raja was the most beautiful girl he had ever seen.

Since Raja's coming to the manor, another large building was being added to the estate alongside the manor, and the two buildings were now called Victory Manor. A drawbridge at the side of the manor was being used to connect the two buildings. More dwellings in the village were also being built in order to accommodate the workers. A lot had already been accomplished in only one year.

Pavel rode in front of the women and shouted, "Victory is mine!"

"Pavel," said Raja. She held out something in her hand. "Please take this."

Pavel moved his horse closer and took a piece of paper from her. He read the message.

Yrotciv si sruoy.

Pavel smiled.

It was their secret code. He felt more empowered than ever. He would win. He would prove himself to everyone at this tournament; he would be the new champion.

The bugle blew again, and the two contestants were on opposite sides of the field.

The crowd shouted, "Show your strength!"

It would all be over in a few seconds. Questions and thoughts filled Pavel's mind. "Will I bring honor to my father and myself or will I fail in defeat? Winning would mean a prize, but losing would mean humiliation. Can I do this at such a young age?"

Immediately Pavel cut himself off from his negative thoughts. "Focus, Pavel, focus. Only think victory. Get your strategy. You can do this!"

In the end, there was one main thing to focus on—hit the target and hit it hard!

Pavel's mind went back to his training. "Rush, yes, that's it. Rush. Rush hard and fast."

He remembered his father's words. "A fast rush for maximum impact. Your opponent will have no time to defend himself."

Pavel's thoughts wandered again. "But the opponent is bigger and older than me. He is known to be the best."

"Today is your defeat!" shouted the other jouster with his war cry.

Pavel gained control of his thoughts. His energy surged as he shouted and thrust his lance in the air. "I will show my strength! Victory is mine!"

Pavel remembered his father's instructions to stay confident and only focus on the task ahead. His expert riding skills could win him this competition. His horse was also the fastest horse his father had ever owned.

The bugle sounded. The riders charged. Pavel spurred his horse into a full gallop. He held his lance steady with precise balance. Sitting himself against the high back of his saddle, he leaned slightly forward. His eyes were fastened on his target. He would get to his target first.

Then smash. Pavel's lance hit hard. The impact vibrated into his bones. Another smash. Pavel's opponent had also hit him. The riders had passed each other and were still on their horses. Pavel's hopes rose.

The two lined up again. Pavel thought to change his strategy. The bugle blew.

The young lord galloped forward, but not at full speed.

At the last second, Pavel squeezed his horse's sides with his legs. The horse lunged forward at great speed. He aimed his lance for the center of his target. He knew he would feel the jar, but he wanted to win. His lance hit. Pain shot through his arm. His opponent was pushed back to the side of his saddle and fell. He had been caught off guard and had no time to aim his own lance.

The crowd cheered. Hankies and flowers were thrown onto the field. Raja held out a red rose. Pavel galloped up to the ladies and took a bow from on top of his horse. He reached for the rose and then placed it between his teeth. He rode around the field with the rose in his mouth and his red and white flag waving.

The crowd hollered with laughter. That was definitely one thing Raja liked about Pavel—his great sense of humor. But, she couldn't help feeling there was more to his antics than just humor. The rose in his mouth was a kiss on her lips. She held her fan in front of her face to hide her blush.

Pavel cantered to the center of the field. He took the rose from his mouth and shouted, "Victory is mine!"

The crowd cheered some more.

Later that day, at the manor, he would join in a ceremony for the young squires. Being the new champion, he would be given a new squire position by his own father, who was knight and lord of the manor. Then he would be presented with his tournament prize.

Chapter 12

Squire of the Body

Pavel sat two chairs down from Raja in the large hall where the dubbing ceremony was taking place. He had liked the rose and the note she had given him. He thought it would be fun to pass her a note as well. He caught her attention and gestured for her to look behind her chair. He held out a note. She took it.

Raja opened the note and read it to herself.

Lla liah ssecnirP ajaR!

Raja smiled.

Lord Viktor raised his voice above the noise of the crowd. "To the brotherhood of squires and knights, we proclaim your life's journey of valor and honor."

A hush fell among the crowd of knights, squires, ladies, and noblemen. Pavel caught Raja's eyes and smiled. She quickly looked away, feeling a little flustered by his attention.

"Yesterday, some of you were dubbed as squires," said Lord Viktor. "Today, you have shown your strength. But you have not reached a mere destination. Rather, you have taken another step along your predetermined path. Let us celebrate these squires and acknowledge their virtuous path, which will no doubt be filled with obstacles and dangers." Viktor raised his goblet and shouted, "Victory!"

The guests around the banquet table stood and shouted, "Victory!"

"We have also gathered here to honor one among us, our new young tournament champion, who will now pledge in front of everyone to walk this path with dignity and humility. Sir Pavel, come forward to receive your dubbing as Squire of the Body, earned by the most skilled tournament player."

Pavel rose from his place. He walked and stood in front of his father.

"I am proud of you, son," said Viktor. "Please kneel."

Pavel bent down and kneeled on one leg. A red and white garment was placed over his shoulders. His father stood back.

"I now call upon Princess Raja, daughter of the tzarina, to come forth and carry out the order of the Squire of the Body."

Raja stepped away from the table and walked toward the area of the ceremony. She walked gracefully and carried an air of confidence but with a display of gentleness. Her hair was adorned with her scarf, and her green emerald radiated from on top of her pale skin. Over the year she had been at the manor, she had grown from a timid peasant girl to a young woman of rare beauty and confidence.

"Princess Raja has come to us out of captivity from a life that was not her blood. She has been rescued from the minds of corruption and deceit that took her away from her royalty and hid her from her true identity. Let us protect her and watch over her with all diligence and truth." Lord Viktor again raised his goblet and shouted, "Long live Princess Raja!"

The crowd repeated the words. "Long live Princess Raja!"

A long sword was given to Raja. She held it in the palms of her hands and then spoke in a clear, loud voice. "The order of the Squire of the Body is presented to you today. Squire Pavel, are you willing to become the Squire of the Body for your own father, the highly skilled knight?"

"I am."

"Squire Pavel, as Squire of the Body, will you always seek to do what is right without reward?"

"I will."

"Squire Pavel, are you willing to stand by your knight in battle, rescue him if he is captured, and carry him if he is injured?"

"I am."

"Squire Pavel, will you, by your conscience and in the eyes of God, strive to keep your thoughts and deeds pure, so God may say, 'Well done, faithful servant'?"

"I will."

Raja then took the sword in her right hand and placed it on Pavel's left shoulder. "For honor," she said. Raja lifted the sword and placed it on Pavel's right shoulder. "For strength," she said. Raja lifted the sword once more and placed it back on Pavel's left shoulder. "For courage. Arise. I now pronounce you Squire Pavel of the order of the Squire of the Body for Lord Viktor."

Pavel stood tall and handsome. The crowd clapped and cheered. Lord Viktor took the sword from Raja and continued his speech. "Now, let us honor Sir Pavel with his well-deserved prize."

Raja moved to sit down again, and Pavel politely offered her his assistance. In the next second, a knife whizzed by Pavel, striking his father. Viktor let out an anguished cry and fell to the floor. Women screamed. Men shouted and shuffled around Raja and Pavel to protect them. Others rushed to Viktor, bending over him to attend to his wound and stop the bleeding.

The people became chaotic. They wanted out of the room. It was difficult to see who the felon was as people were screaming and pushing. Then it became apparent. Someone wearing a black hood pressed through the crowd. He ran out of the hall and then across the drawbridge. His horse was waiting with another horse and rider. He quickly mounted and the two escaped.

"We will go after them!" shouted Pavel as he pointed to the riders galloping away from the manor. He quickly called the names of three knights. Their horses were retrieved, and the four of them chased after the felon.

They would have to ride a long way before they were able to decipher anything of the situation. They rode along dirt roads and then down numerous paths that went through the woods. Finally coming to the edge of a valley, they could see in the distance.

"There they are," said Pavel.

"Look, young lord. They have others with them," said one of the knights, whose name was Arhip Zoruben.

"Yes, a group of warriors, perhaps from the northern regions. They have come well-protected. We cannot continue our pursuit because there are only four of us, and we would surely perish. Let's turn back."

"I didn't notice anyone from the north at the ceremony," said Arhip.

"Me, neither, but it could have been someone else who is not from the north, but who is riding with them. Earlier today I noticed a black horse, strong and not a speck of white on it. Look—do you see it now on the hilltop? His cape and horse are both black."

"I do. The only black horse among all smaller white horses," said Arhip. "I have a suspicion it is the Dark Prince."

"Let's get out of here," said Pavel.

Pavel, Arhip, and the two others rode at a trot back to the manor. When Pavel arrived at the manor, he went straight to his father. Pavel's mother was sitting beside his father, talking softly.

His father responded, "No, dear, it is nothing to worry about. Jealousy always has a way of showing up, but it will subside. There is no need to worry."

"Do be careful Viktor."

His mother saw Pavel enter the chamber.

"Pavel, are you all right?"

"Yes, Mother. How goes it, Father?" he asked.

"I'll be all right," said Viktor. "The knife struck my arm. Maya stitched the wound, and it shouldn't take too long to heal. What did you find out?"

"Warriors. I think they are from the north. But the felon may be of a different descent."

"I suspected that there would be northern warriors involved by the make of the knife, but from what I saw there were no northern people at the tournament."

"But what would they want with you, Viktor, or why would they want any of us?" asked Maya.

Viktor spoke kindly to Maya. "You have to remember who is now here and how she came to us. Raja's evildoers never wanted Raja to be found out. She was intended to be a peasant all her life and to die a peasant. But by a miracle she has been rescued. She is the next heir to the throne, which for some reason seems not to be favorable with her enemies. They want to take her and defeat the throne anyway they can."

Viktor reached over and held his wife's hand and continued speaking.

"I know that danger has been brought to our family. But we must now trust more than ever and make ourselves stronger in order to stand against this enemy. We must protect ourselves."

Maya had tears in her eyes.

"Don't worry, Maya, God sees all. Pavel, alert our guards to keep a more vigilant watch from now on. And you, yourself, keep an eye on Raja."

"I will, Father," said Pavel. "I will forever be faithful to the order of the Squire of the Body."

Chapter 13

Grand Prize

Raja and Pavel were sitting on wooden benches in the courtyard engaged in conversation.

"You want to do what?" asked Pavel, somewhat taken aback.

"I want to learn to joust," said Raja matter-of-factly.

"Girls don't joust," said Pavel.

"And why not?"

"Well, because, it is, well, very dangerous, for one thing," said Pavel, wondering why he was having this conversation in the first place.

"Dangerous, dangerous," said Raja. "How is it dangerous if you teach me? It is only a sport that the two of us will play, and I'm sure you will not be hard on me. Besides, you said it yourself, I have a gift for riding."

Pavel rubbed his forehead and considered the argument. It was true. He had been teaching Raja how to ride and was surprised at how well she commanded her horse. However, he had never heard of a girl-jouster.

"We have already stretched the rules and have allowed you to ride astride rather than sidesaddle," said Pavel.

"And very wise of you since riding sidesaddle is quite dangerous. You said a man's saddle would free the rider from the horse if one should encounter a riding accident. Have you not heard of the recent riding accident of Lady Elvera? Her body was locked into the sidesaddle, and her body was trapped underneath her horse when it fell."

"Yes, yes. She broke her back. Devastating. This fashion of sidesaddle needs to change."

"Precisely, and the tzarina herself now rides astride and advocates it."

"True," said Pavel.

"Very well, then. We have not stretched the rules. We are only doing what is safe for me when riding and what is in support of safety for other girls."

"I do agree with what you are saying."

"Well then, my argument is that jousting may one day save my life."

"I should hope it would never come to that."

"You may hope, but what will come is not up to us. Our duty is to be prepared."

Pavel looked into her eyes. He could sense she was very serious about the matter.

"Besides, Pavel, what harm could a little excitement and exercise do? I want more than just doing what a princess should do. I want to experience all of life. Of course, I appreciate the protection you and your father's knights are providing, but I do not want to feel helpless. I want to feel that empowerment as you do."

"You do have a very convincing argument. But if I agree, you have to promise me one thing."

"What is that?" asked Raja.

"Promise me that you will never lose your grace."

"I promise. I will never stop being a princess."

At that moment, Pavel thought her red hair went perfectly with her beautiful, pale, and flawless skin. The scarf, intertwined in her braid, blended perfectly with the color of her hair. His thoughts were interrupted.

"And speaking of being a princess, isn't it I who commands you? So, Pavel, I, Princess Raja, instruct you to teach me how to joust." And with that statement, she stood tall and pointed her finger straight to his face but could hardly hold back a smile.

Pavel grabbed her hand and thrust it away.

"Spoiled. Downright spoiled, I would say." Pavel laughed and he too stood up straight, a hand's length above her.

With that, Raja grabbed his hat and ran away with it. Pavel chased her until she finally gave up. Out of breath, the two laughed and joked over the situation. Who really was in authority here? They didn't know.

"By the way," said Raja. "What did you get as a prize for winning the tournament?"

"I was granted land."

"Land, that sounds a little boring."

"Quite the contrary. Land is very valuable. It is actually a large estate with a manor and castle on it. It is not run by anyone right now, but I plan to establish it. A knight can become wealthy by owning estates and eventually building his own army. And it was given to me by the tzarina."

Raja looked at Pavel in surprise.

"I see. Perhaps I could visit it sometime then."

"I think I could arrange that," said Pavel as he put his hand to his chin in thought. Raja could tell he had something more to say. "That was not the only gift I received," he said with some lightheartedness in his voice.

"What is it? Tell me."

Pavel smiled. "First, you must do something."

"Pavel, no, please tell me," said Raja, with a pleading look.

"Ah, I need you to agree to this first."

"Okay, what is it?"

"Do not tell anyone I am going to teach you to joust."

"What!" said Raja. "Do you really mean it?"

"Yes, I do."

"You have my solemn promise," said Raja with the most sincere look she could muster.

"Okay then, follow me," said Pavel.

Pavel and Raja walked through the courtyard, dodging some of the chickens that were pecking their way across the yard. Several servants bowed or curtsied to them as they made their way to the outer court where the stables were located.

Raja was now accustomed to the stables. She often went there to talk to the horses. She would give them each a treat, but for Pavel's shimmery reddish-brown horse, she always gave it an extra treat. She couldn't get enough of looking at its white mane and tail.

"Why are we here?" asked Raja.

"You'll see."

They walked on and stopped at one of the end stalls. Raja was stunned. There, standing in the back of the stall, was the most beautiful horse. She had never seen one with such an exquisite color: a very light chestnut with a white mane and tail. The horse looked incredibly stately.

"This horse is magnificent," she said.

"That it is, and a remarkably swift horse as well. It is bred from the best. Its stature is well sought-after."

"This is a grand prize," said Raja with admiration in her voice.

"Indeed," said Pavel, "and it is yours."

"What!" said Raja.

"Yes, I am giving it to you."

Raja stared in disbelief. Here was her very own horse, and a swift beauty at that.

"Thank you," she whispered. "I am very grateful and will care for this horse with great diligence."

"I know you will," said Pavel. "I have seen how you connect with horses, and I feel it is one of your great talents. It's perfect for jousting."

"Did you know that was what I wanted to do?" asked Raja.

"I had an inkling that was your ambition," said Pavel.

Raja smiled. "You are getting to know me too well."

"I hope not," said Pavel. Raja could feel a bit of heat in her face. Pavel noticed and quickly spoke to avoid any embarrassment. "May I continue?"

"Yes, go ahead," said Raja with a slight smile.

"One needs armor to joust, and I would daresay my armor would not fit you."

"Well, a girl always thinks ahead," said Raja with an air of confidence.

"Mmm, how's that?" asked Pavel.

"I arranged with the bailiff to secretly have a suit of armor made for me by the blacksmith at Kazan Castle. The bailiff was a little unsure of my request, but I assured him he would be rewarded."

"Well, is that so? You do think ahead and are quite bold." Pavel grew serious. "Which bailiff was it, the younger one or the older one?"

"The older one."

A little hesitant in his response, he asked, "What do you think of him?"

"Well, I can't say that I have thought about it much. Why do you ask?"

"Oh, it's just something about him that causes me to be suspicious."

"What is it?

"He's too much of a wanderer and he seems to stare at you."

"Maybe it's just that he's very quiet," said Raja. "And it is only your imagination."

Pavel considered the explanation. "Perhaps you are right. What reward are you thinking of giving him?"

"I said I would put in a good word for him to the lord," said Raja.

"Like what?" asked Pavel.

"That he's always on task."

Pavel chuckled. "Always on task to get your armor you mean?"

"You might say that."

"I can see you are determined to get your way with the jousting."

"That I am," said Raja.

Intrigued with Raja's firm and independent spirit, he grew very curious about what she did with the suit of armor. "Where, may I ask, is your suit?"

"It is hidden at my mother and father's tiny house inside the courtyard."

A playful smirk crossed Pavel's face.

"And how do you propose we get it out of there?"

Raja smiled. "I have a plan, but we must wait until tomorrow."

Pavel could not protest. There was something a little exciting about the whole idea. Getting to know this princess was rather entertaining.

Chapter 14

Suit of Armor

Raja sat at her mother and father's table in their little house inside the courtyard of the manor. In a way, it seemed like old times again, except Raja's mother was now healthy and her face relaxed. Her father was much more peaceful and confident, and he always had a gentle spirit toward her. Raja felt relaxed around what she considered to be her true parents. When she was in their presence, she didn't really feel like she was an heir to the throne. She just felt like one of them.

Their house was next to the bakery, and they both worked there. They mostly made bread and had to get up early in the morning to start their tasks. It could get very hot in the bakery, but it was still so much better than the village life they had been used to.

"It is so nice you are here this morning," said Yana.

"You usually don't come this early," said Antom. "I think you must have some news to tell us."

"Well, not exactly news. But I do have a request," said Raja, looking earnestly from one parent to the other.

"Out with it then," said Antom.

"Pavel has agreed to teach me jousting, but I must find a way to get my suit of armor out of your house, so no one sees. I fear if I am found out it would be a disgrace."

"You are right about that," said Yana. "No woman should joust, let alone even want to joust. Are you sure you want to continue with this?"

"Absolutely," said Raja. "I have the support of Pavel. I have convinced him that I may need it someday for my own protection."

"I should hope not," said Antom. "God forbid."

"Raja, do you want some pottage and an egg for breakfast? And how about some goat's milk? There are also some leftover strawberries that you brought yesterday," said Yana.

"Yes, please. I'll have everything."

The three continued chatting and worked to prepare the breakfast. They talked about all the recent events that had occurred and their concerns over the recent near-fatal incident during the dubbing ceremony. Then Raja told them about Pavel's prizes, and how he had given her his horse. She described its beauty and swift ability.

"I'm looking forward to seeing you ride that horse," said Antom with pride.

"Thank you," said Raja.

"Now, for the rest of the plan as to why you are here," said Antom with hands on his hips.

"Of course," said Raja. "Here it is, but don't say a word about it to anyone. Tonight, I will need two-dozen eggs and cheese, as usual. After I come to get the food, you must stay here to help with our breakaway."

"A 'breakaway,' is it?" asked Yana. "We'll see about this in the end."

Raja half-smiled, but then went on to explain her whole plan. Included in her scheme were also the friends of her parents who lived in a little house at the other end of the courtyard. Yana and Antom listened with interest and with a bit of amusement. They wondered if it would really work, but they agreed to go along with the idea anyway.

That evening after the sun had set, Raja knocked on the house of her friends Xenia and Boris. Raja had continued her friendship with them after she had asked that the family be moved into the manor. A little house had been built for them which was now conveniently located near the outer court.

The door opened and Raja quickly went into the small house. She changed into peasant clothing. The three friends brought their scarves close to their faces so as not to be recognized.

"I feel like a villain," said Xenia.

"Me too," said Boris.

"Nonsense, we are like Robin Hood giving to the poor," said Raja, with assurance. "Come on, let's get going."

The three of them met Galina, who escorted them through the manor toward the entrance. Galina acted as if everything was normal so as not to arouse suspicion. She leaned over toward Raja and said in a quiet voice, "Raja, you know I should tattle on you, don't you?"

"Oh, Galina, you wouldn't, would you?"

"Well, if trouble should befall me then you are to blame."

"Rest assured I will take all of the blame."

Pavel was there at the entrance to open the doors and lower the drawbridge. The three of them ran across the bridge and disappeared into the dark. Raja had made this trip before, as she at times secretly stole out in the evening and went to the villagers to give extra food to the very poorest.

Back at the manor, Pavel had waited a little while and then hurried to find his father. He shouted, "Raja is not in the manor. We must look for her right away!"

Surprised, Viktor asked, "How can that be?"

"I don't know, but she is not in the manor."

"Gather two knights, and we will look for her until she is found," said Viktor.

"At your command," said Pavel.

Pavel spoke with two knights. The servants brought horses for Pavel, his father, and the two knights, and they rode into the night to search for Raja.

Viktor gave instructions to the knights, and the four of them split up. Pavel then re-entered the manor using the drawbridge at the side of the building. He went into the courtyard and to the house of Antom. Pavel rushed into the little house.

"Quickly, Antom, help me get the armor to the stables."

"At your command."

Pavel and Antom carried the suit of armor in several bags. They crossed over the moat at the back of the castle and went into the court stables. Pavel secured the bags to the saddle of the horse and covered them with a draping. He then mounted his horse and rode out of the court.

Heading down the Cabane Path, Pavel rode toward his childhood tree house. He thought it was the perfect spot to hide the armor. But only Raja would have thought of something like that. At times, he would wonder why he was doing all this, but at the same time, he thought it was rather exciting, and of course, mischievous.

It was done. The armor was in the tree house. It had been a bit of strain to haul it up the tree, and the bag had ripped in several places, but Pavel's strength proved to be enough to complete the task. So far, the plan was working. No one would suspect a girl's armor was hidden in a tree house, and when she was jousting, if people weren't being too observant, she could be taken for a boy.

When Pavel got back to the manor, he saw that the knights had returned.

"Have you been up to something?" asked Arhip.

"What do you mean?" asked Pavel.

"You know what I mean. I don't think you were thinking. Perhaps some sort of misguidance?" asked Arhip, with a little smile. "Take a look for yourself."

Pavel strode to the great hall. Raja, Xenia, and Boris were sitting with Viktor and Maya. The three young runaways looked serious and repentant.

"So, tell me again why you are running around at night, young lady," said Viktor.

"Surely you can understand," said Raja. "I used to be one of them and I know their desperation. It is harsh to live their life. I only wanted to help."

"And I commend you for your kindness, but this is not a way to solve something you see as a problem. It is far too dangerous for you to do this. You must stop immediately. Is this agreed?"

"Yes," said Raja.

"And I suspect you had Pavel up to something. Is this true?"

"Well . . . I feel that . . ."

"Ah, and here is Pavel standing with us," said Viktor, as he looked at his son. "I think I will have to have a conversation with you."

"Yes, Father."

"Raja, you may go now," said Viktor.

"Thank you, but first I have a request."

"What is it?" asked Viktor, feeling a bit irritated.

"I would like gifts of food to be given to the villagers each week, and also sleeping pallets for those who do not have one. Some villagers do not have furniture or adequate clothing and need supplies to make these things. I would also like for them to have updated farming equipment."

Viktor could not say no to the requests as Raja was princess, and on the other hand, Viktor was not opposed to more kindness shown to the peasants. His income and resources had increased considerably since the arrival of Princess Raja.

"Very well, I will make all of these arrangements for you, but in the future I would like you not to do things behind my back."

"I apologize," said Raja.

"Very well. You are dismissed to go back to your chamber, and Xenia and Boris will go back to their house."

The three of them did as they were told, and Pavel and his father were left alone.

"Pavel, I think you have some explaining to do."

"Well, ah, yes, I admit that I do."

"What else are you are not telling me?"

Pavel cleared his throat. "It was Raja's idea."

"As I suspected, but you are to be the example. I think we need to have a long discussion about it."

There was discussion and debating long into the night, and talk about the Order of the Tzarina and the Squire of the Body. Pavel realized his mistake for allowing Raja to be put at risk. He agreed to be more protective in the future. But finally, a resolution was made, and in Pavel and Raja's favor, she no longer had to hide her suit of armor in the tree house. Permission was granted for her to learn the art of jousting. When Antom and Yana heard about the whole affair, they chuckled about it for days after. The girl definitely had spirit, and there would certainly be a reason for another jousting tournament.

Chapter 15

Kuzma Basnya

Not surprisingly, word about Raja learning to joust had eventually gotten to the tzarina. And contrary to what some would have thought, she allowed it. In fact, she must have approved because she sent another suit of armor for Raja that was lighter in weight. But not to neglect Raja's feminine side, she also sent a gift of several beautiful dresses. Raja wondered what her real mother looked like, and when and if she would ever see her.

Along with the dresses, there was a note emphasizing the importance of keeping up her studies and music practice. Raja had been keenly diligent in all of this and had made quick progress in learning to read and write several languages. This was mostly because of the storyteller, who had moved from the village into the manor.

Raja's musical playing was also a delight to listen to and was another one of her many talents. She was, at this time, in the music room practicing some of her pieces with Pavel.

She plucked the strings of her harp in a merry melody as she sang to her tune.

"A jolly sound," said Pavel. "Play a folk song."

"If you play your balalaika."

"Sure," said Pavel as he picked up the triangular instrument. He had become quite talented at playing the balalaika over the past year and a half, and the two of them together were very entertaining. They often played for the entire household of the manor. The two carried on a lively song.

"Ah, that was good," said Pavel, as he put down his instrument. "You have a very lovely voice."

Clapping erupted from outside of the room. The storyteller, whose name was Kuzma Basnya, came around the corner and into the music room still clapping his hands. "Bravo," he said.

"Thank you," said Raja.

"Do you mind if I join you?" asked Kuzma.

"Not at all," said Raja.

Kuzma picked up his own balalaika, and the three of them played another lively folk song that ended the song with laughter and joking.

"Not bad for an old man, wouldn't you say?" said Kuzma pretending to be old.

"Oh, come now, you're not old," said Pavel. "You do a lot more than most people. I think you can do more than people who are younger than you."

"Ah, well, maybe that's what keeps me young then."

"I'm sure of it," said Raja. "But I think it's also your kind heart."

"'Tis true, pleasant words are good for the bones," said Kuzma with outstretched arms.

Raja laughed. "That's very good. I'm going to take your advice because I want strong bones."

"Wise, very wise," said Kuzma with a chuckle.

"And why are you in such good spirits?" asked Pavel.

"The lord has honored my request."

"What request is that?" asked Pavel.

"Raja should know about it. I am going to Demarcus to see someone about a dream that I had."

"Yes, I remember you telling me about it. It was the dream about the glowing sphere. A monk had a vision that you were supposed to tell this to a certain person."

"That is correct," said Kuzma.

"When do you leave?" asked Pavel.

"In about one month."

"Let us know the day so we can bid you farewell," said Raja.

"I will." Kuzma bowed.

Pavel cut into the conversation.

"Is it time for another jousting lesson?"

"I thought you would never ask," said Raja excitedly. "Yes, let's go. Kuzma, would you like to watch?"

"Not now, my princess. I have work to do."

"All right, maybe next time."

Kuzma agreed to the proposal.

Raja ran up to her chamber and had the maids help her dress into her lighter armor that her tzarina mother had sent. The cloak was made from thousands of metal rings that provided protection, but allowed flexibility in riding and maneuvering the lance.

It was somewhat heavy, but Raja was progressively getting used to it.

Raja's maids escorted her to the entry where Pavel had her horse waiting. She mounted her golden chestnut, and the two rode off to the playing field along what they called the Ajar Path.

"Look, Pavel, no hands!" shouted Raja as she dropped her reins and rode using only her legs.

"You've caught on to that well," called Pavel. "Now pretend you are holding a lance and then thrust."

Raja imitated the technique.

"Very good. I think you shall do well to ride with your lance at our practice."

When the two reached the playing field, Pavel gave Raja her lance. She took it with a display of confidence. Today, Pavel intended to show her how to strike her target.

"Hold your lance close to your body and place your hands against the metal cone," said Pavel. "That way your hand won't slide up the lance when you hit your target. Focus your lance on your target and at the right instant, strike it hard to the target."

Raja caught on to Pavel's instructions and succeeded in knocking the straw-filled enemy to the ground. She turned her horse around to see the approval of Pavel. She continued to practice her skills.

"I don't know what to say. You have caught on considerably well. Shall we have ourselves a little tournament today?"

"A fine suggestion," said Raja, with a wide smile.

The two aligned their horses opposite each other. They held their specially-made practice lances in place.

"Go!" shouted Pavel.

They galloped like thunder toward each other. Raja struck and hit. Pavel raised his lance in approval.

"Again!" shouted Pavel.

This time Pavel struck Raja. He hoped it hadn't been too hard. Raja was prepared and deflected the strike with her shield. She managed to stay on her horse. Pavel was impressed with her balance.

The two practiced numerous times until Raja was quite tired. She didn't think she could maneuver one more thrust of her lance.

"Time to go?" asked Pavel.

Raja didn't have time to answer. Her horse reared and bolted. An arrow had shot by in front of it. She gripped its mane as it galloped away. Pulling on her reins, she tried to stop her horse, but could not. It was too strong. It kept at a full gallop, and Raja was completely out of control of her horse. All she could do was to try and stay on.

Pavel galloped after her. He, too, felt helpless. The path was narrow, and the only thing he could do was stay behind her. He saw a clearing up ahead. This was his chance, Pavel thought. He would move ahead of her and try to slow her horse down. But his effort was useless. Raja's horse was too fast.

Her legs were weakening. She didn't know how much longer she could hold on. Her horse raced around a corner and then another. The manor was in the distance. She knew her horse would gallop to the manor. Desperately trying to stay on she leaned forward. Slipping to the side, further and further, she feared she would fall off. It was no use. She could not hold on any longer. She fell and rolled on the ground.

Pavel came to a full stop ahead of her. He turned his horse and came to her side. He quickly dismounted.

"Are you all right?"

Raja slowly opened her eyes. "I think so, but I'm a little sore."

"Come on. Let's get you on my horse."

Pavel leaped back on his horse and helped pull Raja up as she swung her leg over the back of the horse. Riding double with Pavel brought back memories of when she was first rescued from the fields. Now, he was rescuing her again. Pavel galloped his horse toward the manor.

When they got there, Raja's horse had already been taken care of. Pavel quickly sent orders to search for the villain, and a group of knights set out to find the culprit.

A few hours later, they returned with a peasant warrior. Viktor was sure he was from the northern region. When asked about the incident, he denied it. However, the arrow feathers he carried were the same as those Pavel had found in the field after the arrow had nearly hit him. There seemed to be no doubt that the warrior was the guilty person.

Viktor had the villain locked in a room inside the manor. In the morning, he would be escorted to Kazan for trial and probably executed. People were on edge, and nobody slept well that night knowing that someone dangerous was in the manor.

Morning finally came, but to the lord's horror, the peasant warrior had escaped. A meeting with the guards and the other servants was immediately called. It was then discovered that the storyteller, Kuzma, was missing as well. Viktor had recently appointed him as his new reeve, whose job was to help oversee the estate. The finding was alarming. And the other terrible news was that the older bailiff was missing. The bailiff was always to report his own comings and goings, but now he was nowhere to be found. The meeting with Viktor, Pavel, and a few of the trusted knights continued with various opinions in the matter.

"Father, what do you make of this?" asked Pavel.

"Either Kuzma and the bailiff were both spies or only the bailiff was a spy, and somehow managed to use Kuzma to help the villain escape."

"I can't imagine Kuzma being a spy," said Pavel.

"I agree," said Viktor. "If the bailiff was a spy, they may have taken Kuzma with them as hostage or even killed him."

"My guess is," said Pavel, "that they took Kuzma as hostage."

Arhip, who was listening to the different versions of what could have happened, offered his explanation. "It could also be possible that the bailiff was bribed by the villain to let him escape, and they took Kuzma with them. Kuzma could be worth a fair bit of coin."

Pavel thought about the odd behavior of the bailiff. "I didn't trust the old bailiff. I think he was probably in on it."

"You could be right, Pavel," said his father. "Above all, I think Kuzma is innocent and we need to get him back."

The others agreed to this last opinion. Pavel also thought to himself that there certainly wouldn't be any need for Raja to put in a good word for the bailiff now as she had promised. Pavel knew he would be the one to have to tell Raja about Kuzma. He wasn't looking forward to it.

When Raja heard the news about her beloved storyteller, she cried. He had been a very loyal friend and had uplifted her spirits whenever she was down. Just yesterday, he had been so happy that he was allowed to make the trip to Demarcus. Now, it seemed that it would never happen.

Raja would miss Kuzma's storytelling. His tales had been a delightful treat for her. They were always so compelling. And she marveled at all the languages he knew and the fact that he was teaching them to her. Now there would be no one to do that. But Raja determined that she would continue to practice everything he had taught her.

That evening, Raja took her doll and turned it over in her hands to comfort herself. She remembered the night Kuzma had given it to her. The gift was beautiful in her eyes. Raja counted the twenty-four pearls, remembering how Kuzma had asked her to count the little doll's fingers and toes, and the pearls, to ensure she remembered the numbers. The memory brought tears to her eyes. She kissed her doll. It was still perfect. She vowed do everything she could to get Kuzma back.

Chapter 16

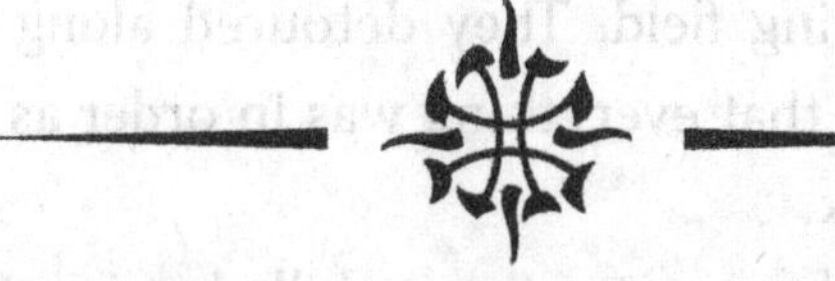

Keeping Score

Search parties were sent out to find Kuzma, but not a trace of him could be found. After several months, the searches subsided, and it was presumed he was no longer alive. Raja couldn't believe deep inside of herself that he was gone forever. She somehow knew he was still alive and waiting to be rescued. She believed that someday he would be found.

Since the incident that had happened during Raja's practice jousting session, Viktor had increased security measures. The tzarina had sent more than double the number of knights to help secure the manor. A careful watch was taken with anyone leaving or coming to the estate.

Over the course of several more months, Raja continued to practice her jousting. She became progressively stronger and more skilled. Raja insisted on keeping score, and there were several competitions when Pavel thought he had let his guard down too much and had to concentrate to bring his score back up. In fact, there was a time when Pavel claimed that Raja had won. Raja didn't really believe him and just thought he had allowed her to win. But Pavel insisted it was true.

Raja and Pavel talked together on their horses as they rode back from the playing field. They detoured along the fields of wheat, making sure that everything was in order as the peasants tended to their work.

"Raja, you really have gotten very skilled at jousting. I'm sure no one could tell your skills apart from any boy-squire."

"Thank you," said Raja. "I've had an excellent teacher."

"I have something that I think you would like to hear."

"What is it?"

"There is going to be a jousting tournament at my estate in three months' time."

"Oh, and are you saying that I'm invited to join?"

"Well, only squires are allowed to participate, and you are not a squire yet."

"But you say I have all of the skills. Could there be an exception?"

"I don't know. The rules are quite strict."

"I have an idea."

"You always have an idea," said Pavel, with a chuckle.

"I could ask my tzarina mother, and if she says yes, then I could participate."

"You are crafty, aren't you?"

"Sometimes," said Raja, with a smile.

"Well, you better get that letter out soon then."

Pavel rode his horse away from Raja. He turned to the side to cup his hands over his mouth.

"I hear an owl," said Raja. "Where is that coming from?"

Pavel made the hooting sound again.

"It's you!" said Raja.

Pavel laughed and made a wolf cry.

"For that, I'll race you to the manor," said Raja, hoping to give him a challenge.

"As you wish."

They galloped like the wind up the hill to the manor.

Raja won by a full horse length.

"How did you manage that?" asked Pavel, feeling out of breath.

"Well, it just so happened that you gave me your swiftest horse," said Raja.

"Ah, that I did. I guess it is my fault then."

The two of them laughed and made their way into the manor for the evening meal. While sitting at the long table during the meal, Lord Viktor discussed the plans for going to the tournament at Pavel's estate, which was north of the manor.

Viktor addressed his son. "The playing field at your estate is more suitable than the one here because of the large plateau that the castle is situated on. I'm expecting a lot of participants."

"How is it going to be organized?" asked Pavel.

"The tzarina is sending servants and knights to your estate to get ready for the tournament, and we will do the same. Galina will be the head servant. The manor is very large and can host a lot of people at once. We won't be using the castle."

Raja hoped she would be able to participate in the tournament as she listened to Viktor's plans. She reasoned that the tournament was very important to her mother as she was sending her own servants and knights. Perhaps she would be able to meet her at the event.

"Does the tzarina attend the tournaments?" asked Raja.

"She does, but she won't be attending this one," said Viktor.

"I was hoping she would be there."

"Yes, I can understand that, which brings me to a point that I was intending on sharing with everyone."

Not wanting to take her next bite of food until she heard what Viktor had to say, she waited patiently for him to continue.

"I have received a letter from the tzarina stating that under the circumstances she will not attend the tournament, but instead, she has requested that we make plans to have Raja go to Kazan Castle to meet the tzarina in her own castle rather than on a jousting field."

Raja's eyes widened, but before she could speak, Viktor held his hand up. He spoke in a slightly serious voice looking at Raja. "Kazan Castle is to the east of here and it is a hard four-day journey, a much longer travel than to Pavel's estate. Do you think you could manage that?"

Barely keeping her composure, Raja quickly stood up. "You are asking me if I can manage a four-day journey? Of course, I can." Tears of joy flooded her eyes. "It seemed so long in coming, but now it is upon me. I am finally going to meet my blood mother!"

Maya stood up and gave Raja a hug. "I'm so excited for you," she said as she looked into Raja's face.

Wiping the tears from her face, Raja said excitedly, "We must schedule more training sessions to meet my tzarina mother. She must not be disappointed."

Raja stepped away from Maya to display her forms of curtsies, which were already well practiced. Then catching everyone by surprise, she took Maya by the hand and danced around the room with her. "Was that a yes?" asked Raja.

"Yes, of course Raja," said Maya as she swirled under Raja's arm and then turned to face her. "But, we shall talk about it later when you are a little more calm."

Chuckles came from Viktor and Pavel as they watched Raja and Maya dance around the room. "I think we need to continue our conversation," said Viktor.

Raja and Maya curtsied and then sat back down at the table. Galina, who had been quietly watching from the kitchen entrance, gave Raja an encouraging smile. Everyone seated was now silent and attentive before Viktor continued.

"We will start early in the morning and take three knights for protection. We will ride along the Hillock Trail going into the Hemencurcle Valley. The valley is flat so it should be easy riding and only take us one night to arrive at our first destination, which is the western part of the hillock range. There is a stream there to refill our water skins. After that, we will continue through the range on the same trail into the slopes of the Trough Valley. We should arrive at the estate in the evening of the third day."

"Do we wear armor?" asked Raja.

"Of course," said Viktor. "We must be protected at all times, and you especially, being the princess. You have exceptional skills, but nonetheless we will protect you with our lives." Viktor looked at Maya and continued. "Maya, you will stay here at the manor to attend to its affairs. Guards will be posted at all times for your protection."

"Thank you," said Maya. "I will wait for your return."

"Good, we shall make a return in about two-weeks time. And then of course we will make plans to go to Kazan Castle."

"I shall work at preparing for that journey," said Maya.

Viktor nodded to show approval and then addressed Pavel. "Make sure we have ample supplies of food. We will leave in three months' time."

"Yes, Father, I will see to it."

"Good. If everyone has finished the meal and there are no more questions, you are dismissed."

"Thank you, Father," said Pavel. "Raja, would you like to ask Xenia and Boris to join us in a sword-fight practice?"

"I most certainly would," said Raja, with a slight air of supremacy.

Pavel noted her attitude with a little smirk. "I see I will have to make our practice a bit more challenging to keep you in check," he said, with a smile.

"Try as you will," said Raja, "but I'm a tough one to take on." She stepped aside and thrust her arm out as if fighting with a sword.

"That you are," said Pavel. "Run to get your friends before the sun goes down."

Raja ran to the courtyard to call upon Xenia and Boris. They immediately said yes to the proposal, and all four met in the courtyard. Each person had a wooden sword and a shield for practice. They took turns competing against each other and kept score with pebbles.

Boris had natural talent, and it was challenging for Raja to keep ahead. They were tied for a good portion of time, but eventually Raja won the game. Xenia surprisingly loved the sport and wanted to practice as much as she could. She even wanted to follow in Raja's footsteps and learn how to joust. Raja agreed that after Xenia mastered riding with no hands she could begin learning how to joust. Boris wanted to be taught as well and would not let up until Pavel agreed.

Finally, the four had their fill of the sword-fighting practice.

"Well, who won?" asked Pavel with an air of satisfaction.

"Okay, we know who won," said Raja. "But you do have a few years on us."

"Just wait until I'm older," said Boris. "Watch me surpass you."

"Ah, we'll see about that," said Pavel.

"I don't think we'll see about that. I think I know. I'm already challenging for anyone here."

Pavel certainly detected a good deal of competitiveness in Boris. He thought his combative nature was good, but at the same time he did not want to lose a friendship with Boris over sword fights. He would make sure to keep an eye on that and cultivate a proper attitude in the coming months. Boris had a determined nature, and when he wanted something he did not let up.

"So, Pavel," said Boris, "I hear you are going to a tournament."

"That's right. How did you hear?"

"Word gets around fast when my sister is best friends with the princess," he said.

"I see," said Pavel, "and no, you cannot come."

"But I do not see why not. I have been inducted into the Order of Page, and I would help with everything. There would be a lot of knights who would need help. And I would learn how to be a squire that much quicker."

"You can learn it here," said Pavel, speaking with some authority.

"I have something that would be of value for the journey," said Boris.

"What is it?" asked Pavel.

"My eyesight is better than most, and I could detect trouble before others."

Pavel thought Boris had a good point, and after a bit more discussion, he finally agreed that Boris could come to the competition. "But promise to stay out of trouble."

"Me, get into trouble? Not me," said Boris.

Pavel slapped Boris on the back in friendship and then proceeded to find his father. The rest of the evening would be spent in sword-fighting practice with his father. For the practice, they used real swords with blunted edges. Raja kept score, but as usual asked to join the matches. Pavel could never say no to her. As a result, Raja was becoming an excellent swordswoman.

Chapter 17

Not the End

Raja rode her stately horse cocooned inside the troupe of armored knights. Each knight carried a lance, shield, and sword. Their horses wore trappings with ornamental displays and contrasting colors. The knights were proud of their skills, their accomplishments, and of their duty to protect Princess Raja.

Pavel and Boris rode bravely beside each other. Pavel could certainly have been mistaken for one of the knights, but Boris definitely still showed his boyhood. Pavel's duty was to keep a close watch on him. Everyone's main concern was to arrive at Pavel's estate tournament safely and in good time.

"How long have we been riding?" asked Boris. "I feel thirsty. Can we stop at the stream?"

"Not yet," said Pavel. "Concentrate on the course. Don't forget why you came."

Boris looked ahead at the northern part of the Hemencurcle Valley. The land had a gentle roll, spotted with rocks and shrubs. The hillocks could be seen in the distance, which curved around the valley in the shape of a horseshoe. Boris kept his keen eyes on the hills. A group of wild horses dotted the landscape. They could have been mistaken for a small army but Boris' eyesight could make out the difference. But, to Boris' right-hand side, he saw a different type of movement. Speechless for a moment, he couldn't get his words out.

"Pavel . . . Pavel, there, do you see it? Movement on the hills."

Pavel squinted through the haze of the sun to make out the moving objects on the side of the hills. "People?"

"Yes, riders with horses."

"That could mean danger," said Pavel.

"I'm counting about fifteen in the group. And they've started a gallop."

Pavel could see the dust pick up in the air.

"Father!" shouted Pavel. "Up ahead on the hills. Over there to the northeast."

Viktor, leading his armed forces, stopped his horse. He gazed along the side of the hills.

"Looks like a group of warriors," he said, "and heading this way."

"Perhaps coming to greet us," said Arhip.

"Let's hope that is the intent," said Viktor.

Viktor continued to lead his knights toward the hills. The two opposing groups grew closer. It didn't take long to see that the warriors of the approaching groups were large and intimidating. Some wore pointed helmets. A metal band ran between their eyes, attached to a chain link mask. The slits in the masks were dark and daunting. The armor they wore was a mismatch of metal and peasant clothing. A few of them carried a lance with a shield.

The armed groups stopped a fair distance from each other, forming a line, and faced each other.

"We are the Zurkians. Who are you?" shouted Viktor.

"We are the Tyhets!" shouted the chieftain.

Viktor knew of the Tyhets. They were from the north and known for their expert horsemanship and fighting skills. Viktor noticed that some of their armor was similar to that worn by the warrior who had been captured near the manor.

"I think these may be the warriors responsible for shooting that arrow in the playing field," said Viktor to Pavel. "Look at their arrow feathers."

"Not hard to determine that. The big warrior in the middle seems to be the leader."

The Tyhets were rebels of the country and fiercely independent. They didn't let anything stand in the way of getting what they wanted.

Pavel sat uneasy in his saddle. He hoped that whatever took place in the next moments Boris and Raja would be safe. He cast a look at Boris and then looked back at Raja. Both of them didn't seem to be letting on any fear. A good sign he thought.

"You have plenty of room to go around!" yelled Viktor.

"We don't go around!" shouted the Tyhet chieftain.

"What do you want?"

"You have a princess. We challenge you to a test of your loyalty and bravery."

Viktor was not a coward, but he did not want to put Raja or Boris in danger. He did not trust the Tyhets.

"We do not wish to take your challenge. Please move aside."

The Tyhet chieftain yelled. "Then it will be known that you are a mockery of the throne, and do not wish to strengthen your skill. You are not fit to protect your princess! Accept our challenge to prove your fearlessness and faithfulness."

Viktor thought quickly. If he didn't fight, it could mean shame and mockery and the Tyhets in the end might challenge him despite his request. If he was right, he would have an advantage by being the first to charge.

"Urra!" shouted Viktor and moved his horse forward at a full gallop. The others followed beside him.

"Fear in your lowly state," shouted Pavel.

"Today is your defeat," shouted Raja. She held her sword to the side of her body, slightly pointing it outward.

Lances hit metal, and riders fell from their horses. The Tyhet chieftain, who was on his horse, challenged Raja with his sword. Fighting hard with all of her strength, Raja clashed her sword against his, but her opponent was much stronger and she was knocked from her horse.

Viktor was hit hard from behind and fell. Picking himself up, he was immediately challenged to a sword fight by a Tyhet. Other knights and warriors around them were fighting back and forth with swords.

Then Pavel, who was battling with his lance, fell when his opponent struck hard. He turned to get up and saw Raja picking herself up from the ground. The Tyhet chieftain dismounted from his horse and challenged her with his sword. She was determined to show her bravery and blocked his blows with her shield. The impact of his blows resonated pain through her body, right down to her bones. She turned a circle and swiped her sword against his with a powerful blow. He was impressed, but his smile was devious.

Quickly moving in Raja's direction to help her, Pavel lost his footing and fell to the ground. And in that second, the Tyhet knocked the sword from Raja's hand and pinned her to the ground.

"No one moves, or your little princess dies!" shouted the Tyhet chieftain as he held a sword to Raja's chest.

Boris was also pinned to the ground by another mean-looking warrior. "They both die!" yelled the warrior.

The chieftain looked at the mean-looking warrior. "Shut your mouth. I'm the one giving orders here."

Viktor held up his hand to stop his knights from further attack. The sword fighting stopped.

The chieftain looked into Raja's face with mockery.

Raja gritted her teeth. She was breathing heavily. "You won't get away with this."

"Who's holding the sword, Princess? It's not you or your lord. Can't you see it's me?"

"Not for long," said Raja.

"On the contrary, it will be for a long, long time."

"Let her go!" shouted Viktor.

The chieftain laughed. "I got what I came for!"

"The wrath of the throne will cut you down like a scythe in a grass field!" shouted Viktor.

The chieftain yelled, "And you will be trampled like a rodent under a stampede of wild horses." He commanded his warriors to take Raja. "Get this princess off the ground and onto her horse!"

The warriors grabbed Raja. She struggled, but her struggles were quickly put to a stop. She was hoisted onto her horse and surrounded by the Tyhet riders' swords.

"No one follows us or she will die!" shouted the chieftain. "Not that I would want to kill such a beauty, but those are my orders!"

Viktor shouted back. "This is not the end! You will be defeated!"

"I am warning you! Do not come after us!" shouted the chieftain. And with those last words, Raja's seized horse was led away and the group of warriors galloped off toward the western hillocks.

Raja turned her head to look at Viktor's group of armed men, which grew smaller and smaller in the distance. Feelings of fear overcame her, but she fought to push them away. She knew deep down inside that these Tyhets would not get away with their evil plans.

Viktor's knights picked themselves up and mounted their horses. Viktor looked on with seething rage.

"Go after them, Father!" yelled Pavel.

Doing his best to control his emotions Viktor responded with a stern face. "No, not yet. We will go to the hillocks and wait until just before sunset."

Viktor gave his commands and his group rode their horses at a walk until they got to their destination. They dismounted and allowed themselves to eat the food they had brought.

"There has been a constant threat to Raja's safety, and now this," said Pavel, as he spoke to the group around a small fire. "But why do the Tyhets want this princess?"

"Perhaps the Tyhets and the Dark Prince are in alliance," said Arhip.

"Ah, the Dark Prince, who is uncle to Raja, and wanting the throne. Yes, he could be using the Tyhets to gain his own power," said Viktor.

"But what could the Tyhets gain from this?" asked Pavel.

"Granted, they are against the royalty, but I'm sure the Dark Prince could think of some benefit for the Tyhets—probably bribery," said Viktor.

"What is your plan, Father?" asked Pavel.

"We will get her back at night."

"Should Boris come?"

"Boris, do you want to come?" asked Viktor.

"Yes, I will come," he said, trying to sound older than he was. The attack had been scary, but he didn't want the others to think he was cowardly in any way.

"Good," said Viktor. "Here is the plan."

Pavel and Arhip listened with intensity and added their own ideas to the well thought-out plan. They would start the search right away while the tracks were still visible, but would have to make sure to keep a safe distance away from the Tyhets. The knights would stay at the camp and wait for their return.

Pavel thought of how terrified Raja must be feeling. He hoped with all his might that she was safe and unharmed. Somehow, though, he knew that Raja would have a deep sense of trust beyond her fear. Her life was here for a reason, and she would come out alive. Pavel would see to that, even in the face of any danger.

The Tyhets may have succeeded in capturing her, but this wasn't the end. Viktor and his men would succeed in rescuing Raja and defeating the Tyhets in their treacherous scheme. With those thoughts, Pavel's hope and determination grew, giving him a strong sense that they would come out victorious.

"Granted, they are against the [illegible], but I'm sure the Dark Prince could think of some benefit for the Tybets—probably bribery," said Viktor.

"What is your plan, Father?" asked Pavel.

"We will get her back tonight."

"Should Boris come?"

"Boris, do you want to come?" asked Viktor.

"Yes, I will come," he said, trying to sound older than he was. The attack had been scary, but he didn't want the others to think he was cowardly in any way.

"Good," said Viktor. "Here is the plan."

Pavel and Arbin listened with intensity and added their own ideas to the well thought-out plan. They would start the search right away while the tracks were still visible, but would travel to make sure to keep [illegible] away from the Tybets. The knights would stay at the [illegible] to wait for their return.

Pavel thought of how terrified Rela must be feeling. He hoped with all his might that she was safe and unharmed. Somehow, though, he knew that she would have a deep sense of trust beyond her fear. Her [illegible] for a reason, and she would come out alive. Pavel could see to that, even in the face of any danger.

The Tybets may have succeeded in capturing Rela, but this was not the end. Viktor and his men would succeed in rescuing Rela and defeating the Tybets in their treacherous scheme. With those thoughts, Pavel's hope and determination grew, giving him a strong sense that they would come out victorious.

Chapter 18

The Search

Viktor, Pavel, Arhip, and Boris set out in their search to find Raja. The horses' hoof marks that led west between the hillocks were relatively easy to follow, and they were making good progress. Viktor knew the Tyhets had headed toward the river, but he suspected it could present a problem.

Viktor was right. When they reached the river, the hoof marks stopped. The warriors no doubt walked in the water along the shoreline and came out somewhere down or up the river. The problem was that this shallow shoreline went on for a great distance. If they took the wrong turn, it could cost them ever finding Raja again.

"Which way do you think they traveled?" asked Pavel.

"Logically speaking, downstream, because from what I know, the Tyhets live in the northern regions," said Viktor.

“South would be upstream and is toward Dracon,” said Arhip. “They may be involved with the Dracians since the Grand Padesha had mentioned his involvement with them.”

“And it is possible that they could meet a ship along the river to take them to Dracon,” said Viktor.

“But I think we should travel north. In my way of thinking, they would want to get to their settlements as quickly as possible for reinforcements,” said Pavel.

“I think you are probably right,” said Viktor. “Let's head north.”

The four of them turned their horses to head north. Pavel's horse was not responding as well as it usually did. He turned his horse around again, but the horse refused to move forward.

Viktor rode back to Pavel. “Son, lean forward more, and let the horse know who is boss.”

“I don't think I need to be told how to ride,” said Pavel. “I know how to ride. My horse is just acting strangely.”

“Give me your reins and I'll lead him to get him going.”

“I think I can manage. He might just need a bit of time.”

“We don't have time. Give me the reins.”

Pavel looked up and sighed at his father's interference. He was just thinking of complying with his father's wishes when he noticed something fluttering in the trees upstream.

“Someone is in those trees,” said Pavel pointing with his finger.

Viktor, Arhip, and Boris instantly looked in the same direction. They saw it too, but it was not a person. Boris saw that it was something else. The four of them decided to investigate it. Pavel's horse had no problem going in that direction. Cautiously, they rode upstream until they got closer. Then everyone saw what it was, a scarf hanging loosely on a branch of a tree.

Pavel rode closer and took it from the tree. "This is Raja's scarf!" Everyone was astonished.

"If I know Raja, she took off her scarf and hung it here in hope that we would see it and know which way to go," said Pavel.

"Well, it worked," said Viktor. "Come on. Let's head this way."

The four of them now headed upstream instead of downstream. Pavel stuffed the scarf inside his armor. He shivered at the thought that they had just about made the wrong turn. Had Raja not made it her tradition to always wear her scarf, the rescue group would surely have gone the wrong way. But Raja had always felt the scarf was special and that she needed to wear it.

The group kept moving, listening and looking for any more signs. They found none. The sun had long set, and it was now almost too dark to ride. It would be dangerous to ride in the dark as the horses might stumble or spook. If they spooked they could either bolt or make unwanted noise.

"Let's go a little farther and then stop for the night," said Viktor.

The others agreed and found a spot to rest. Pavel listened to the night sounds. He heard the sound of an owl in the distance. He loved the sound of owls. It made him feel relaxed. But relaxation right now wasn't something he wanted. He hoped with all his might that Raja was okay and unharmed. It was torture to think how terrified she must be. He knew, though, that she was praying for help.

Then suddenly, it came to him—the owl calls. There were three short hoots and then a long one, and there—it happened again. It was coming from the direction they were headed, but a little to the east.

Pavel woke his father. "Father, they are close by. I heard owl hoots. But I'm sure the owl hoots are coming from Raja. It is a signal that she practiced with me, and I recognize it. The hoots came from over there."

Viktor heard it too. Then it stopped altogether. The four huddled together and made a plan. They drew diagrams in the dirt to clarify their plans. There was discussion and some debating and, finally, a decision was made. They left their horses by their small camp and set out on foot to find Raja. Relief came to all of them knowing she was probably still alive.

Chapter 19

Mockery Overturned

Looking around at the warriors encircling the fire, Raja saw that most were lying down and drifting off to sleep. She remembered the imaginative games she had played with Pavel. At the time, it had been very amusing. She never imagined she would be in those same scenarios in real life. But now she was using those very tactics she had only used for fun. She hoped her owl hoots would be heard and recognized.

"I'd like to walk around a bit," said Raja.

"You just did that," said the mean-looking Tyhet.

"What is that to you?"

"You are up to something."

"I assure you, I am up to nothing. What could I do?" asked Raja.

"Let her go," said the Tyhet chieftain as he gulped down some liquid from a red bottle.

"Give me some of that," said the Tyhet.

"It's mine. And don't think of taking any of it or you're dead."

Raja wondered what sort of liquid was in the red bottle as she watched the chieftain gulp down the solution. It ran down his chin and left a red stain.

The mean-looking Tyhet made a disgruntled face and then took out his frustration by yelling at Raja. "What are you looking at?"

Raja put her hand up to stop his yelling. "Don't yell at me."

The Tyhet gave her a mocking sneer.

Raja put her hand on the log, ready to help herself up.

"I'm going to sleep," said the chieftain. "Make sure the girl does not escape." The chieftain leaned over and put his knife to the Tyhet's neck. "And keep your own hands off of her. The orders from the Dark Prince are that she is delivered to the Dracians unharmed."

The Tyhet wiped his nose as if to say he wasn't concerned about the chieftain's orders.

Now standing, Raja listened to their conversation.

"How would the Dark Prince ever know?" asked the mean-looking Tyhet.

"He'll find out from the khan of Dracon after Raja gets there." The chieftain pointed to Raja, who was listening to every word they were saying. "The khan won't accept this princess under any other circumstances. We don't want anything to stand in the way of us getting our coin from the prince."

The mean-looking Tyhet laughed. "It was funny to see the prince angry with the padesha. Those stupid Odyhuns couldn't even find her. Luckily for us, we can do the job for the Dark Prince."

"Just don't get too confident. It's not done yet."

"It will be," said the mean-looking Tyhet.

Feeling annoyed, the chieftain asked, "Do you know you have a mean-looking face?"

Getting back at the chieftain, the Tyhet said, "Not as mean as yours."

Then, wanting to have the last word, the chieftain said, "Have you looked at yourself in a mirror?"

"No, have you?"

"Once, but I don't any more. But I think you look meaner."

"Well, good for me then," said the mean-looking Tyhet.

The chieftain burped. "If you say so."

Thinking this would be a good time to leave the fire, Raja walked a short distance away from the camp. The Tyhets didn't seem to be watching her all that closely. They were too busy nattering at each other.

"Why don't you look at yourself in a mirror?" asked the mean-looking Tyhet.

"I don't like mirrors."

"Why not?"

"They're hexed."

"How do you know that?"

"My face looked distorted."

"How do know it wasn't just the mirror?"

The chieftain yawned. "I'm not taking chances."

The Tyhet and chieftain quit talking and in a short time, they fell asleep.

Walking to the edge of the bushes, Raja put her hands to her mouth to make an owl hoot. Suddenly she was grabbed and a hand went over her mouth. She wanted to scream but couldn't.

"Shhh, don't scream." She knew it was Pavel.

"Pavel," she whispered, feeling very grateful. "I knew you'd find me."

"We have untied all of the Tyhet's horses and have led them away. They are waiting for us downstream. Come on. We must hurry."

Pavel heard the cry of a wolf. He hoped it was Boris. No one would be able to tell the difference between Boris' wolf cry and a real wolf cry. He was particularly good at mimicking the sound.

"Did you hear that wolf howl?" whispered Pavel.

"Very clearly."

"I think that's Boris."

Raja nodded and pointed in the direction from which she heard the howl. Pavel moved ahead in that direction and they began their escape. Every few minutes, they heard more wolf cries, which hopefully kept them in the right direction.

Thankfully, they found the group of horses. Viktor, Arhip, and Boris were waiting for them.

"Good work, Boris," said Pavel.

Boris felt proud he had done something right.

"Is my horse here?" asked Raja.

"There it is," said Pavel.

Raja managed a slight smile.

"Each person will lead a group of horses," said Viktor. "Pavel, you lead the way. Boris will follow, then Raja. Arhip and I will come up from behind."

Viktor and Arhip worked quickly to tie the horses in a train for Pavel. After Pavel went ahead, they did the same for Raja and Boris. Finally, every horse of the Tyhet warriors was trailing behind the five riders.

The only thing Raja heard was the swooshing of the river as the horses waded through the water. She felt exhausted, and her body craved sleep. She caught herself nodding off, but a slight stumble of her horse woke her. She struggled desperately to stay awake.

The water got deeper, and the horses had to put more effort into walking through the water. The current was fairly strong now. Raja felt like her horse might be swept away. The deeper section only made up a short distance, and soon the ride would feel less treacherous again. Raja's horse stumbled. She was caught off guard and fell from her horse into the cold water.

Raja gasped and tried to hold herself steady, but her feet kept slipping, and she was swept away from her horse. She struggled to stand, but couldn't. She was being pulled further into the river.

Pavel slid from his horse and swam after her. He caught her. "Don't panic!" he said.

Raja remembered using those exact words when helping Hannah in the moat. She trusted Pavel and let him help her toward her horse. He helped her up on her horse, and they continued their trek. If Raja wasn't awake before, she certainly was now. She felt cold and hoped this ride in the river wouldn't last much longer.

Viktor and Arhip had seen the event from behind and gave them an approving sign as encouragement to keep going.

The group finally came to the place where they had first entered the river. Viktor had flagged the spot with a tripod of sticks. The sun was just dawning, and he thought they had arrived at just the right time.

"Here is where we can let go of the horses," said Viktor. "We will each ride with just one other horse, and the others will follow."

Viktor and Arhip untied the horses, and the group started the last part of their journey. They began at a slower pace and eventually galloped toward their camp. When they arrived at the camp, he ordered the other knights to mount their horses. They left immediately for Pavel's estate.

In the evening of the next day the group arrived at the estate with the captured horses. They were quickly welcomed and the fleet of horses was promptly put into the stables. The animals would be well taken care of.

Raja was quickly escorted into the manor beside the castle and was taken care of. She was in desperate need of some rest.

Viktor, Arhip, Pavel, and Boris were escorted into the manor hall. They were given food and drink.

"I think we did well for ourselves," said Viktor. "We just doubled our assets."

"I can just see the look on the Tyhet faces when they wake up to see their horses gone," said Pavel with a chuckle.

Arhip smiled. "They are going to have a long walk home," he said.

"Whoever's plan that was sure didn't work out," said Viktor. "I have a sense an abduction won't be happening again for a long time."

"Hopefully, never," said Pavel. He raised his goblet. "Look where the mockery lies now!"

"Indeed," said Viktor as he held up his goblet for a toast.

Everyone agreed and toasted to their victory.

Later that evening, Pavel and Viktor sat down to write a letter to the tzarina explaining what had happened and asking her to forgive them for having been overtaken by the Tyhets; the enemy's numbers had been greater. He explained how Raja had overheard that the Dark Prince was behind the kidnapping. He also explained how the rescue had taken place and how Raja had been instrumental in the success of the rescue. The letter concluded that they would take extra knights with them back to the manor before they journeyed to Kazan.

After the letter had been written and sent by a servant, Pavel found Raja on the top balcony.

"Are you all right?" he asked.

"Yes," she said. "I knew you would come to rescue me."

"You were brave." Pavel brushed a strand of hair from her face. "Here's your scarf."

"My scarf!" said Raja.

"How did it get onto the tree branch?" asked Pavel. "You know, if it weren't for your scarf, we would not have found you. We were about to go the wrong way."

"It was easy," said Raja. "I pretended that I saw a bear, and when no one was looking I tossed my scarf in the tree. No one even noticed it."

"Very crafty," said Pavel.

"Thank you."

Pavel wanted Raja to take extra precautions at the tournament. "Be vigilant while we are here."

"Don't worry. I will look out for myself. I am going to enter the tournament, am I not?"

"I don't know," said Pavel. "You will have to wait to find out."

Pavel turned to go back into the manor. Before he disappeared around the corner, he looked back at Raja. She was wearing her scarf again. She looked beautiful, as usual. He was enamored with her intelligent way of helping him rescue her from the Tyhets.

Later that evening, lying on his hard bed of stone and straw, Pavel felt it was barely enough straw to get any comfort. After rearranging the straw, he put his hands behind his head as he lay on his back thinking about the events of the past two days. He was very thankful that they had been led in the right direction in their search, however, he felt responsible for what had happened and wished he hadn't stumbled during the battle. Surely, then he could have prevented the terrible experience of her capture. Granted, Raja did not seem that affected by the horrible ordeal. Pavel saw her as being furiously strong. He wondered if she thought of herself that way and if she understood where she got her strength. Perhaps it had to do with her being brought up as a peasant, but again, he wasn't sure if that made sense, since when she first came she was very shy. Perhaps it was just who she was. He knew she had a trust in God. He would have to talk to her about her thoughts on that matter and how it affected her. In the meantime, he would have to see about having a more comfortable sleeping arrangement in his manor. He turned and tossed for some time and then, finally, fell asleep out of sheer exhaustion.

Chapter 20

The Order of Squire

The next morning was sunny and calm. Looking out of the window from the top level of Pavel's manor, Raja watched the squires who were practicing their jousting. A dress hanging inside her chamber was waiting to be tried on. She had been looking at it all week wondering if she would end up wearing that or a suit of armor. She knew she should put it on now and sit with the nobility and act like the other women. But she couldn't get her mind off the fact that she wanted to compete in the tournament. It sounded so exhilarating. And besides, after the last dangerous escapade, she needed to gain her confidence back. Pavel had spent time practicing with her during the week on account of the capture, and now she wanted to prove herself to Pavel and Viktor.

"Raja, are you ready to put on your dress? The tournament is about to start," said Galina, with a sigh and her hands on her hips.

"Was there any word in regard to me joining the tournament?" asked Raja.

"No, my princess, none."

"I will call you shortly. I want to be alone for a while."

Raja thought of sneaking into the tournament, but then thought better of it. She had already disobeyed Viktor once and didn't want to make him angry again. She would wear the dress for the tournament. She called for Galina. Her dress did look stunning on her.

Raja walked down to the sit where the other noblewomen were seated. An announcer welcomed the guests and proceeded to call out the names of the contestants. Someone who appeared to be of high nobility rushed up and interrupted him. A scroll was handed over to him. The announcer unrolled the paper and read what was written.

I announce that Raja, Princess of Kazan, will play in the tournament. Signed by the Tzarina Valentina.

Murmurs ran throughout the crowd. Such a thing was extremely rare. Only royalty who had power could ever dare to make such a request. And such was the case now. Raja had just been allowed to participate in the jousting tournament. She was sure her heart skipped a beat at the surprise.

Raja ran inside the manor to put on her armor, with Galina hurrying after her. Galina was an expert at putting Raja's armor in place, and everything was done in very short order.

"I wish you the best," said Galina.

"Thank you," said Raja.

Galina escorted Raja to the playing field. Her own horse was waiting for her. The trappings were exquisite. She had never seen anything like it, and no doubt they were from her tzarina mother. She mounted her horse with pride.

Raja rode out into the playing field to join the other contestants, who were already parading around the arena showing off their horses and shouting war cries. As soon as Raja entered the field, the crowd was ready to cheer her. The applauding and yelling escalated as she cantered around the field with her flag held high and her horse draped in purple and gold.

The tournament was about to begin. A member of each team lined up on opposite sides of the runway. Lances got into place and the bugle blew. The squires galloped toward each other. One player was knocked down, a member of Raja's opposite team. The contest continued. The score was even on both teams. Raja was next.

She held her lance close to her body. The bugle blew. There was no time to think of what to do. She could only believe that what she had learned was enough. A loud crash rang out. Her opponent had fallen. Cheers rose from the crowd. The game continued, and then it was Raja's turn again. She charged and then struck and in the same instant she was struck. It jarred her horribly, but she stayed on. Looking back, she saw her opponent had fallen. Cheers went up again.

Pavel was on the same team as she was, and right now their team was winning by one point. His turn was next. His entire focus was on his opponent. He charged, and his performance proved successful. Their team was up two points. It was now Raja's turn, the last turn of the game.

She galloped.

She missed.

She was struck.

A moan rose from the crowd. She slipped to the side of her horse, but in the last split second, managed to stay on. No one was knocked down. The two opponents lined up again.

The bugle blew and the two riders charged. Raja struck and hit. Pain jarred her body. She looked back and saw that her opponent had fallen. Whooping and cheers went up from the crowd. Her team had won by three points. She lifted her flagged lance and let out a war cry. Her accomplishment was almost beyond her belief. She had done it.

The announcer gave congratulations to the winning team. Then he announced the individual winners with the most points. Pavel was given first place, another squire second place, and Raja was given third place. Pavel couldn't have felt more proud of her at that moment. Her performance had been more than admirable.

Pavel rode up to his father and exchanged a few words. Then he rode over to Raja. "Raja, I have some news for you that I think you are going to like."

"Tell me."

"Tonight you are going to be given the Order of Squire by my father at the ceremony."

Raja's face beamed. "I'm catching up. You just watch me."

"I know, and I'm scared."

"And you have every right to be."

The two laughed and rode to join Pavel's father. As Raja was riding across the playing field, her eye caught a glimpse of something familiar—a girl with a deep hood that hid her face. The girl motioned for Raja to come to her. Raja rode over to the girl.

"Meet me at the stalls," said the girl.

Raja nodded. She knew it was Hannah.

Raja gave her horse away to a stable boy and rushed toward the stalls. She desperately wanted to know why Hannah had come.

Hannah was waiting by her own horse in one of the stalls. "Congratulations, Raja."

Raja gave Hannah a hug. "Thank you. I'm so glad to see you."

"I have good news and bad news," said Hannah.

"What is it?"

"My father has been put in prison for treason."

"Was that on account of my kidnapping?"

"Yes."

"So you heard."

"I hear a lot of things from my father," said Hannah. "It was my lady-in-waiting who had informed the tzarina about his devious plans of kidnapping you. He was so angry that you had escaped he couldn't hold back from ranting and raving about it." Hannah wanted to encourage Raja. "You are brave beyond words to have gone through that."

"Thank you. I cherish your admiration. Please go on," said Raja.

"You are safe for now, but my father has gained power and I think he will eventually find his way out. He has a lot of followers. But I shall always try to keep you informed."

"Thank you," said Raja. Relief swept over her, and for now, she could relax. She didn't know how long that would last, but the one thing she would do was be brave.

"Hannah, have you heard anything about Kuzma?"

"No."

"So you know about him?"

"Yes, and I'm sorry for your loss."

"I'm still hopeful."

Hannah put a hand on Raja's shoulder. "I know."

Raja looked into Hannah's eyes. "Can I see you later?"

"No. I must leave right away. No one must know that I am here. The throne is still at risk."

Raja tried hard not to reveal her disappointment.

"My identity must be kept a secret. Only a few know," said Hannah.

"Does the tzarina know about you?"

"No, not even the tzarina."

Raja looked seriously at Hannah. "I will tell no one."

"You must go now," said Hannah. "But remember we are friends forever."

"I will remember," said Raja. "Take heed."

The two girls departed and Raja went up to her chamber. She readied herself and was escorted to the hall where the ceremony would take place. People rose when she entered. It felt funny, but she knew she would have to get used to it. When she was called for her dubbing into the Order of Squire, she got up and gracefully walked toward the front of the crowd.

Viktor was standing and waiting. She knelt to receive the Order of Squire. Viktor presented Raja with a shield bearing a crown symbol representing victory.

Viktor spoke proudly as he raised the shield. "Raja, I give you this shield as a symbol of your loyalty to the tzarina. May it protect you and our country. God be your help." Then a sword was placed in her hands. He continued. "Raja, this is a special sword given to you by the tzarina. I now give you this double-edged sword as a symbol of your bravery and faithfulness. May it serve to divide the enemy who comes against us. God be your help."

Looking at the shiny metal and the skillfully created angles, Raja decided she would use the gift to serve the tzarina in protecting the throne with loyalty. She confidently walked back to Pavel. It certainly wasn't the custom for a girl to carry a sword and shield, but she didn't care. After all, she was a princess.

Part 3

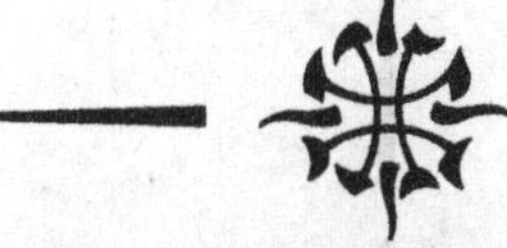

Dracon

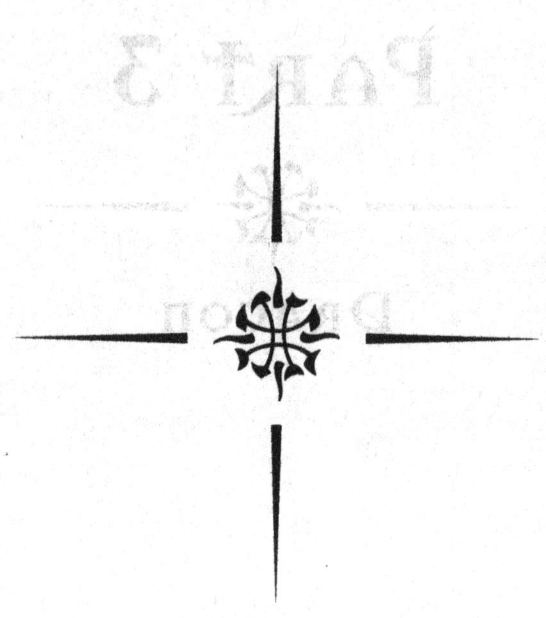

Chapter 21

The Masquerade Ball

It had been a long time since Pavel had ridden to the Village City of Kazan, which was a three-night trek east along the Volga River. Raja was the only girl in the group of knights and squires, but that didn't bother her and she travelled as well as everyone else. She was very excited to see the city, but most of all she could hardly wait to finally meet her blood mother.

When they were close to the city, they first travelled through Kazan Village, which was outside the city gates. The farming peasants lived in the village. Their farmed land looked similar to the land at the manor, but the area was much, much larger, as there were many more plots of land.

Finally, coming to the thick, arched gates of the city, the group found the gates open and they rode into the merchant streets. Making up the inner core of the group, Raja rode closely beside

Pavel and ahead of them were Viktor, Arhip, and Boris. Other knights surrounded the inner group for complete protection.

The bazaar was filled with sellers and buyers from the city village. It was noisy and crowded. The merchants yelled out their wares and buyers bartered using their own goods. Pavel tried to point things out to Raja, but she couldn't hear most of what he was saying because of the noise of the people and the clomping of the horses.

There were too many items to really know what it all was. She noticed some of the larger items, such as the rugs Pavel talked about and furs and silks. There were also carts and baskets with food. She felt like stopping to look at them, but knew she wouldn't be permitted. They were to keep going until they reached Kazan Castle.

Raja saw a few children wandering in the street. In particular, she saw a young boy hiding himself among the traders. Even though his face was dirty, he was cute-looking with blond hair. He took something from a cart and then quickly hid himself behind some people. His clothing was ragged. She wondered about him and why he would steal. She was sure the punishment would be severe if he was found out.

Traders with carts and mules darted out of their way as Pavel and Raja rode through the walled city. They passed a large building, which was connected to other rectangular buildings of various sizes. A large bell tower rose from the center and three loud clangs resonated through the streets.

"What's that building?" asked Raja.

"It's a monastery," said Pavel. "It's where the monks live."

Raja wondered if the monk that had visited Kuzma lived there. She thought it would be interesting to find out. Farther ahead, the castle appeared. It was much larger than the manor Raja lived in. The view took her breath away with its numerous pinnacles, steeples, and turrets. She wondered what the coming evening would be like in the castle.

"What did you say the name of the ball was?" asked Raja.

"It's a masquerade ball," said Pavel. "The tzarina is throwing this ball in honor of you coming to her castle."

"So in other words, my mother is celebrating our meeting for the first time since I was a young child."

"I would say so."

"And what is a masquerade ball?" asked Raja.

Pavel slowed his horse. "I haven't been to one myself, but it's an occasion where people wear masks and costumes."

"That's odd," said Raja. "For what purpose?"

"People say it is more fun when you don't know who everyone is."

Raja smiled. "I think I shall have fun."

Pavel and Raja arrived at Kazan Castle and rode their horses up the arched stone bridge leading to the Soladecorus Gardens. A small stream ran under the bridge and formed a small reflective pool in the center of the garden. Riding to the end of the long garden pergolas, they were met by a group of servants and a lady-in-waiting. Then, after dismounting, the servants led their horses to the stables.

The lady-in-waiting bowed to Raja.

"Please," she said, "this way."

Raja followed her to a large room with a canopy bed. Chambermaids were busy in the room preparing the bed. She saw a row of elegant dresses hanging from an iron bar. Gold necklaces, feathers, and colored jewels were on a dresser beside it.

"Please choose a dress for the ball," said the lady-in-waiting, whose name was Bettalia Bloompetuler.

Raja looked at the dresses. They were even finer than the ones she already had.

"I choose this purple dress. I love the color purple."

"Well chosen," said Bettalia.

The maids busied themselves in getting Raja ready for the ball. Exquisite pieces of jewelry were picked out, and her hair was beautifully woven into a braid using the scarf her mother had given her. Finally, Raja picked out the mask she would wear, red with small, purple diamonds. A sense of excitement and nervousness flooded her.

"You look as fine and as rare as a purple diamond," said Bettalia.

Raja smiled and tried on the mask. It was rather mysterious and fit perfectly. "And this?" she asked.

"You look like a panther prowling at night."

Raja laughed.

"Tis a lovely costume, my princess. Please, sit down. A fine meal will be served to you," said Bettalia.

Raja sat down and continued to look around her. Candles were placed around the room for light and comfort. In front of her, a warm fire glowed in a large round fireplace. The food was served shortly. The menu proved delicious. There were bowls of fruit, stews, breads, and sauces. Raja beckoned the other maids to join her in eating the food.

"Who comes to the party?" asked Raja.

"Anyone can come," said Bettalia. "That is because everyone will be wearing a mask, and no one will know who people are."

Raja still thought that was odd.

"People of lower class can enjoy the party without feeling judged," said Bettalia.

"Okay, that makes sense," said Raja.

"At the end of the ball, people take off their masks."

Raja thought about that as she put her spoon back in the serving bowl. "Would I then see the tzarina?"

"Perhaps," said Bettalia.

"How should I act at the ball?" asked Raja.

"Don't worry about that. It's a masquerade ball."

The conversation continued until Raja was finished eating, and then Bettalia decided the time was right to leave. She and the chambermaids wore masks with a few small feathers, and together they all made their way to the party, which was already well underway. The maids giggled and talked as they walked down the corridors.

Festive music and laughter floated from the hall, and new arrivals were being escorted to the ball. Raja was led through the door. She couldn't believe the sight. Dancing, eating, singing, talking, and flirting were all happening at once. People came with plates of sweets and glasses of wine. For now, she declined all of it. She wanted to know where Pavel was.

The room was so crowded it was extremely difficult to see all the people. There were other boys with long, wavy, black hair. Wearing the masks, they all looked the same to her. A dance had started, and someone whisked her to the dance floor. Dancing had been one of the many things she'd had to learn, and thankfully, she had loved it. The boy she was with had brown hair and was definitely not Pavel. She twirled around and went in and out of people as she moved down the line.

One of the men came in close to her. "Raja, it's me."

"You're hard to find."

"That I am, but you are not."

"Meet me after the dance," said Raja.

"Where?"

"On the balcony." Raja didn't have time to say any more as she was whisked on down the line. The dance was over, and another one started. But before she could reach the balcony to meet with Pavel, a boy stopped her and asked her for a dance. She was obliged to comply, and the dancing started again. She didn't seem to be able to escape the dance floor. She desperately wanted to find Pavel again, but couldn't find an opportunity.

When the dancing was over, there was hardly a chance to catch her breath with girls coming to her and asking her questions, and boys walking by and bowing. Food was offered, and she found herself taking the food and drinking the wine. She was beginning to feel like she was having a good time. She let down her guard and laughed along with the others.

The night wore on, and it was announced that it was time for people to take off their masks. One by one, the masks were taken off, and people revealed their faces. Shrieks of surprise and laughter filled the room.

Raja remembered why she was here in the first place. Where was the tzarina? She looked to see if anyone would beckon her. She felt self-conscious and uneasy as numerous eyes gazed upon her. The party was still going on, but it didn't seem as fun anymore. She turned to leave.

She just wanted to get to her room. Upset, she ran down the hall. She entered her room and flung herself onto her bed. She started to cry. Why had it turned out this way? Why hadn't her mother come to greet her? She cried on her bed feeling frustrated and hurt. She didn't know how much time had gone by when she felt a hand on her shoulder. It was Bettalia.

"Raja," said Bettalia. "I know you must feel upset, but please don't cry. I have a note here from the tzarina. It's for you."

Taking the letter, Raja unfolded it and read it to herself.

To my Dear and Lovely Daughter Raja,

I know you wanted to meet me tonight, but I couldn't bring myself to do that. I have heard that you are beautiful, and I felt exhilarated to see you. But at the same time, I felt guilt. I have waited so long to see you. I didn't want to take you from the life that you knew because for you, the peasants were your real parents. You were already ripped away once. Tomorrow, in the later afternoon, I would like you to meet me formally as your tzarina. We will look upon each other for the first time since you were three years old. Then I will conduct a ceremony and pronounce you Princess of Kazan.

Sincerely, your Tzarina Mother Valentina, who always wishes you much love

Wiping the tears from her eyes, Raja said, "Thank you Bettalia. I'd like to be by myself now."

Bettalia bowed and left the chamber.

Raja read the letter over and over again. She was going to be crowned Princess of Kazan? What would that mean? She wondered if she would stay in Kazan Castle or go back to Pavel's manor. She would talk to Pavel about it in the morning.

and hurt. She didn't know how much time had gone by when she felt a hand on her shoulder. It was Bettula.

"Raja," said Bettula. "I know you must feel upset, but please don't cry. I have a note here from the Tsarina. It's for you."

Taking the letter, Raja unfolded it and read it to herself.

Our Dear and Lovely Daughter Raja,

I know you wanted to meet me tonight, but I couldn't bring myself to do that. I have heard that you are beautiful, and I felt exhilarated to see you, but at the same time I felt guilt. I have waited so long to see you. I didn't want to take you from the life that you knew because, forgive me, the peasants were your real parents. You were already ripped away once. Tomorrow in the late afternoon I would like you to meet me formally as your Tsarina. We will look upon each other for the first time since you were three years old. Then I will conduct a ceremony and pronounce you Princess of Kazan.

Sincerely, your Tsarina Mother, Valentina, who always wishes you much love.

Wiping the tears from her eyes, Raja said, "Thank you Bettula. I'd like to be by myself now."

Bettula bowed and left the chamber.

Raja read the letter over and over again. She was going to be crowned Princess of Kazan! What would that mean? She wondered if she would stay in Kazan Castle or go back to Pavel's manor. She would talk to Pavel about it in the morning.

Chapter 22

Baku

Raja awoke to the song of a bird on her stone windowsill in Kazan Castle. She got up and opened the shutters. The streets already had a few merchants setting out their goods. She thought she would love to wander about and look at all of the things. Then she remembered the boy she had seen. She was curious about him and wanted the chance to ask him why he had stolen something. No young child should be stealing. She would have to wait to talk to Pavel about last night's events and about the note from her tzarina mother.

She called for Bettalia and quickly got dressed. "I'm going to visit the bazaar," she said. "Come with me."

"Why is this so urgent?" asked Bettalia as she laced Raja's corset from behind.

"I saw a young boy on the street yesterday, and I need to find him."

"Why, my princess?"

"I saw him steal, and I need to know why."

"Steal? It's best not to talk to him. You don't want to get involved with that."

"He's just a boy, and I want to help him. And besides, I might want to visit the monastery. I'm very curious about it."

Bettalia wrapped Raja's scarf around her hair and hung the green emerald necklace around her neck. "Are you sure about this? It may not be safe for you to be there by yourself."

"That's why you are coming."

"And a lot of good that would do."

Raja took a piece of fruit that was left from yesterday and put it in her pouch. "I think we are ready. Let's leave."

"At least take this with you," said Bettalia as she handed Raja her double-edged sword.

Raja took the sword and swung the strap over her shoulder. She left the chamber with her maid following her. They both walked to the castle entrance. The doors were open and they unobtrusively walked past the guards. Walking at a fairly quick pace, they went through the gardens and down the arched bridge, then headed toward the village city.

The streets were filling up with people and wares. Raja slowly walked by the displays and carefully eyed all of the contents. She ran her hands over smoothly carved furniture and spindles and sorted through garments of silk. Perhaps she could purchase one of the garments later. She came to an assortment of spices, which had a very strong aroma. She didn't think they had those spices at the manor. The fruits looked wonderful, and she most certainly wanted to test them for flavor.

Then out of the corner of her eye, she spotted a blond head. She knew it was the boy. She moved closer to him. She bent down and looked him in the face. "I want to talk to you," said Raja.

The boy ran into the crowd, and Raja ran after him. Bettalia began following Raja, but very soon she was left behind.

The boy was quick, and he darted in and out of the crowd with ease. But Raja was quick too. She saw him turn down an alley, then around a corner. She ran after him. He disappeared. She slowly walked down the alley, and then behind her, he darted out and ran. Raja turned and ran after him. The boy turned several more corners, and they continued that way for a good while, but Raja finally caught up to him.

She grabbed him and hung on to him. "I'm not going to hurt you. I only want to help you. I want to be your friend."

"What do you want?" yelled the boy.

"I saw you steal yesterday, and I want to know why."

The boy struggled to get free again.

"I have a piece of fruit for you. I'm not going to hurt you or report you. Will you sit up and eat it and tell me your story?"

The boy relaxed and took the fruit. He ate it quickly.

"I can have more of that for you," said Raja softly. "Please tell me your story."

The boy looked into Raja's face, his eyes starting to trust. "I was a slave, but I ran away. I don't know my name."

"Do you have parents?"

"No."

"So you are an orphan?"

"Is that bad?"

"No, how old are you?"

"I don't know."

Raja guessed him to be about eight. "And you are hungry?"

The boy nodded. "I do some things for merchants, but sometimes they don't pay me."

"What would happen to you if you were caught stealing?"

"I would starve to death."

Raja's face turned to a frown at the thought of that cruel punishment. She agreed stealing was wrong, but it seemed the boy had no choice but to steal. He had to eat.

"I will help you," she said. "While I am here, I will meet you in the village and give you some food. And I will try to find work for you from honest people. That way, you don't have to steal."

The boy agreed to that. He looked admiringly into her face.

"I have something that I want to show you," said Raja. She took her little doll from her pouch and gave it to the boy.

He turned it over in his hands. It's pretty," he said.

Raja took off her pouch and gave it to the boy. "Here's my pouch, and I'm going to let you keep the doll in here for a while. This is so you know you can trust me. The doll is very special to me."

"Where did you get it?"

"My friend gave it to me."

"What's your friend's name?"

"Pavel."

"He must be a kind person."

"He is," said Raja.

"What's your name?" asked the boy.

"Raja. I am staying in the Kazan Castle."

"Are you a princess?"

"Yes."

"I've never met a princess."

"I'm sure you haven't."

It started to rain and in no time they would both be soaked.

"I have to go back to the castle. Please don't lose the doll."

"I won't," said the boy and slipped the doll into the pouch.

Raja turned to hear heavy footsteps coming down the alley. A large Tyhet warrior hastened to approach her. Standing in front of her, the warrior shouted, "Get up."

Raja recognized him as the Tyhet chieftain who had captured her before. Seeing his sword pointed at her, she did as he commanded.

"Ah, dressed like a princess. My task at hand will prove to be easy." The chieftain relaxed his stance and a menacing smile appeared on his face.

"I see we meet again," said Raja. "I was hoping it wouldn't take too long."

The chieftain put his head back to laugh and at that instant Raja drew her sword from her back and had the tip at his neck. "Now it's I who holds the sword."

More heavy footsteps echoed down the narrow alley. The chieftain's eyes turned to see who it was. "Not for long," he said. "You better drop the sword or my warriors will kill you."

Three Tyhets surrounded Raja and she dropped her sword. Hitting the ground, it rang like the bell of the monastery. For a moment, there was silence and then in a rough manner she was tied at the hands and gagged at the mouth.

Eyeing Raja's scarf the chieftain scoffed at her. "I should gag you with your own pretty scarf. Then maybe you'd learn not to escape."

With fire burning inside of her, Raja wanted to say he would regret his words.

"Get that one too!" shouted the chieftain. The boy had been sitting wide-eyed and petrified. He tried to escape, but the Tyhet caught him, gagged his mouth, and tied his wrists.

The chieftain ordered Raja down the alley. "Get moving!"

Raja stumbled ahead, her heart beating in time with the pellets of rain falling hard against the cobblestone. Her arms hurt from the tightness of the ropes. What was happening to her? She had thought she was safe, but now she was being led away from the castle toward the tall city wall.

The rope was untied from around the wrists of Raja and the boy, and they were pushed into a dugout hole. The hole led into a tunnel that went under the city wall. The Tyhets forced their captives to move through the tunnel. Once outside the wall, they were put on a horse and covered with hooded cloaks.

"Don't try anything," said the Tyhet chieftain.

Raja knew there was no way to escape and so she obeyed their orders. The group of horses rode away from the Village City of Kazan. They were headed toward the Kazanka River where it intersected with the Volga River. After what seemed like a long time, they arrived at Port Alexandra where a ship was waiting. Men rolled barrels of goods onto the ship. The warriors ordered Raja and the boy to dismount and they were forced onto the ship.

Raja had never even been on a ship, and she was sure the boy hadn't either. This was not the first sailing experience she had hoped for. The Tyhets would not get away with this and would pay for their evil doings. Pavel would come for her.

The warriors pushed them along the ship to meet Captain Mossovince.

"Make sure they get delivered to Baku unharmed. The khan will be waiting for the girl, and he can have the boy as a gift from me," said the chieftain.

"So is it the Dracians who want the girl?" asked the captain.

"You heard right, and don't make any blunders."

"Well, I don't know what I could do to make things go wrong."

"Take it from me. A lot could go wrong," said the chieftain. "She has already escaped once and it can't happen again." He pulled his dagger from his sash and twirled it around in his hand.

The captain's face turned grave. "I understand."

"I'm warning you, she's as slippery as an eel. Don't disappoint me."

The captain nodded.

The chieftain handed the bag of silver coin to Captain Mossovince. He willingly took it. He knew the Dracians had paid a high price for this girl. He commanded his crew to take the girl and boy below the deck to ensure they could not escape.

But right before Raja and the boy were taken, the chieftain pulled the gag from Raja's mouth and held his dagger to her face. "Don't scream or you will regret it," he said, in a snarly voice. "You won't be needing this anymore. You're only a peasant girl." And he ripped the green emerald from Raja's neck.

The chieftain's mean face sent chills through her body. Then a deep sadness filled her heart, and tears welled in her eyes. He couldn't take her mother's crown jewel. No, that was a gift. He just couldn't do that. "You can't take that!"

"How did you get this?" asked the chieftain.

"It was given to me by my mother," said Raja.

"By your mother," said the chieftain. "That's what I thought. This must be a crown jewel."

"Please don't take it. It was a gift!"

"Like I said, you won't be needing it anymore," said the chieftain. "Gag her and put her and the boy in the hold!"

A crew member jerked the cloth back onto Raja's mouth. The chieftain and the warriors turned, disembarked the ship, and were gone. Defeated, Raja and the boy were forced down into the hold of the ship. They were each tied to a post and left in the dark.

Chapter 23

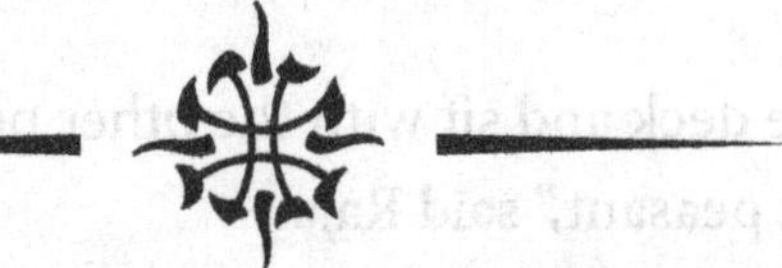

Asleep in the Aftercastle

A loud groan echoed through the wooden hold of the ship. Raja felt the ship rock and thought it must be moving out of Port Alexandra.

Raja tried giving some comfort to the boy by making eye contact. He was frightened, but still in control of himself. The ropes gripped her wrists, digging into and burning her skin. Her muscles ached from being in one place and she hoped she would not have to stay like this for much longer.

The air smelled musty and pungent. Raja couldn't quite decipher the smell, but thought it came from the barrels. A cluster of small sprigs with tiny light-green leaves stuck out from underneath the lid. Furs and fossils were stacked around the barrels and a heap of shed caribou antlers were in the middle of the hold. She also noticed a pile of bows and arrows in the far corner.

She shuddered as a rat ran across the floor. She hoped the rats wouldn't come anywhere near her.

The trap door was lifted, and light filtered in from above. The captain climbed down the ladder into the hold, took the gags away from their mouths, and untied the ropes that wrapped around their wrists.

"Go to the deck and sit with the other peasants," he said.

"I'm not a peasant," said Raja.

The captain snickered. "What are you then?"

"I'm a princess."

"A princess? Well, we'd all like to be a prince or princess."

"It's true. Ask the boy."

The boy nodded in a convincing manner. "She is telling the truth. I have her doll to prove it." The boy gave the doll to the captain to look at.

Looking at the doll, the captain said, "It does look valuable."

"And look at what she is wearing," said the boy.

"It is a beautiful dress, but that still doesn't prove it."

"Listen to this," said Raja and she spoke some words in different languages.

Rubbing his chin, the captain looked at Raja as if he almost believed her. "You're just about convincing me, but to say that you are a princess is a little too hard to believe. You don't have to be royalty to know more than a few languages."

Raja desperately wanted to prove her identity. "Give me something to read."

"Sure," said the captain. "But the joke will be on you."

Captain Mossovince left and came back with a book. He handed the book to Raja in a nonchalant manner. "See if you can read this."

Opening the book, Raja saw that it was a navigational book. The text was very familiar to her, as Kuzma and Pavel had spent time teaching her things about the sky. She began reading the text and explaining what she knew about telling direction with astronomy.

Raising his eyebrows, the captain said, "I admit you are well educated, but if you are a princess what are you doing here? It doesn't make sense to me."

Raja explained how she had discovered her true identity, but how her life was in constant danger on account of it, precisely because her jealous uncle wanted the throne. She told the captain about Lord Viktor and how she had just ridden to Kazan with the lord and his son, Pavel, to meet her tzarina mother for the first time. Then she explained how she had found the boy and that she was just about to go back to the castle, but instead, the Tyhets captured her.

"I could possibly believe your story because I know who Viktor is, and what you have said about him is true," said the captain. "But what am I going to do about your situation? My life will be in danger next if you are not delivered to the khan of Dracon. So I'm afraid I can't help you, princess or not."

The captain was about to go back up to the deck but Raja shouted at him. "Stop! Don't leave! If you help me, my mother will reward you substantially."

The captain turned around to face Raja with one foot on the first rung. "That wouldn't do me any good. If you aren't delivered, the Tyhets would find me, take my reward for themselves, and then kill me."

Raja knew she had to offer more. "You will have protection!"

"What kind of protection?"

"You will live in the castle."

"How do I know this is what the tzarina would do?"

"She is a ruler of integrity."

Furrowing his brow, he considered the offer. "How much reward?"

"You will never have to work again." Raja could see she was convincing the captain. "You can hide the boy and me on the ship and when we arrive in Dracon you can say to the khan that I never entered the ship. Then you can take us both back to Kazan and we will immediately go to the castle. You must have a good hiding place on this ship."

"As a matter of fact, this ship does have a hiding place that only I know about. I think that might work. It's in the aftercastle, which is my sleeping quarters."

Raja was relieved. She would go back to Kazan, and an end would be put to this constant threat on her life. The tzarina would have to now deal with it.

"Sit on the deck for a while, and at night you and the boy can sleep in my cabin."

"How many nights will this take?" asked Raja.

"Three nights, including this one, and we should be there, but it also depends on the wind and the rowing crew."

Raja turned to the boy. "I will call you Fedor."

"Okay," said the boy. "I like that."

Raja and the boy climbed out of the hold and sat on the deck with a group of three young peasants. There were two boys and one girl. Raja sat beside the girl, who looked about the same age as she was. "What's your name?" asked Raja.

"Shamra Loza."

"I see that the river is getting quite a bit wider. What is the name of this river?"

"The Volga."

"Are you being sold?"

"Yes."

The girl was actually pretty and had beautiful blond hair. The color was much like Fedor's. She had a solemn look, and Raja remembered what it was like being a peasant, but this situation seemed much worse—the experience of being sold like an animal. They were human just like anyone else. It shouldn't be this way. Why did someone else get to decide the life of another human being?

"Do you have parents?"

"I don't think so; I was living with my aunt. I had a younger brother, but he was taken when he was a very young boy, and I don't know what happened to him."

"That's terrible," said Raja..

"It was."

"What happened to you now?" asked Raja.

"During the night, they came to Kazan Village and I was taken away from my hut. My aunt was hysterical when it happened."

Raja wished she could rescue the girl. She wanted to tell Shamra her own story, but couldn't deal with the pain she was feeling. "What happened to your mother?"

"I don't know exactly. I was very young, and my aunt never wanted to talk about it."

"I'm sorry to hear that."

Shamra appreciated the comment, but given the present situation she thought it didn't matter anymore.

The Volga River was becoming wider and wider, and in the next hour they were in a large body of water. Raja couldn't even see the shoreline. "What water is this?" she asked.

"It's called the Khvalyn Sea. And we're headed south to Baku."

"Where is Baku?"

"Baku is in Dracon. That's all I know."

Of course the Dracians would live there, and from what Raja remembered of Pavel's descriptions, she did not like the Dracians. She hoped her plan would work.

It was getting dark. Captain Mossovince came over to Raja and the boy. "Follow me," he said.

Raja and Fedor followed him to the stern of the ship and then to the aftercastle. The captain opened the door of the tower-like structure. "These are my sleeping quarters. You may sleep here."

Raja looked at Fedor. He seemed to like the idea. *Like a boy,* she thought.

The two were extremely tired and didn't have a problem falling asleep, especially with the rocking motion of the ship. She had tried to discover where the hiding place was in the aftercastle, but failed to find it. She was sure the captain would show her tomorrow morning.

Raja and Fedor were fast asleep in the early morning. However, escaping anyone's detection, the ship was being swarmed by men climbing up the sides and onto the decks. Pirates crept around the deck and to the sleeping quarters of the crew, capturing everyone they came across. Raja's door creaked open.

"Well, look what we have here. If it isn't the captain o' the ship."

Raja and Fedor woke with a start. Fedor screamed. The man showed Raja his cutlass, and she retreated to the wall.

"Get up and onto the deck."

They obeyed. On the deck, every crewmember was held hostage, with the captain in front. A rope cinched the captain's neck. The pirates collected the crew's weapons and threw them into the galley boats that floated alongside the ship. The captain was forced to order his crew to hand over the ship's cargo to the pirates. The galley boats were filled with the goods.

"Pirates," whispered Raja.

"I'm scared," cried Fedor.

"Don't worry; I won't let them take you."

The pirate captain eyed the young peasants and yelled, "Take all of the peasants!"

Fedor clung to Raja.

"Who's that one over there?" asked the pirate captain.

The captain said nothing. A pirate tightened the rope around the captain's neck.

"Speak!" yelled the pirate captain.

"She's a princess from Kazan," he said, in a raspy voice.

The pirate captain yelled, "What else?"

"The khan of Dracon is waiting at the Port of Baku for her."

"Ah, Baku, land o' the Dracians. I'm sure the price was high fer that red hair."

The rope was tightened around the captain's neck again.

The pirate captain shouted to the ship captain, "When ye get t' Baku, be sure t' tell the khan his slave princess be on Kulaly Island!"

Raja and Fedor were shoved along the ship's deck. Fedor started to cry, and the two of them were forced into one of the galley boats. The pirates left the merchant ship and rowed their boats toward the pirate ship, with its black and white skull and crossbones flag flapping in the wind.

into the galley boats that floated alongside the ship. The captain was forced to order his crew to hand over the ship's cargo to the pirates. The galley boats were filled with the goods.

"Pirates," whispered Kala.

"I'm scared," cried Tedor.

"Don't worry. I won't let them take you."

The pirate captain eyed the young peasants and yelled, "Take all of the peasants!"

Tedor clung to Kala.

"Who's that one over there?" asked the pirate captain.

The captain said nothing. A pirate tightened the rope around the captain's neck.

"Speak!" yelled the pirate captain.

"She's a princess from Kazam," he said, in a raspy voice.

The pirate captain yelled, "[illegible]"

The [illegible] of [illegible] [illegible] the Port of [illegible] for [illegible]

[illegible] land [illegible] the [illegible]. For sure the [illegible] was high [illegible] that [illegible].

The [illegible] the captain's neck again.

The pirate captain shouted to the ship captain, "[illegible] [illegible] [illegible] this slave [illegible] be on [illegible] Island!"

Kala and Tedor were shoved along the ship's deck. Tedor started to cry, and the two of them were forced into one of the galley boats. The pirates left the merchant ship and rowed their boats toward the pirate ship, with its black and white skull and crossbones flag flapping in the wind.

Chapter 24

Beauty

Fedor sat close to Raja, trying to stay warm. Shamra and the two other boys sat on her other side, and together they nestled in the corner of the pirate ship's deck.

"I'm scared," said Fedor.

"Me too," said Raja. "But remember, I'm a princess, so I don't think they will harm us."

"What did you say?" said the older boy. "You're a princess?"

"Yes, I'm the daughter of the tzarina."

"I see. So this is all your fault then," said the older boy. "Now we're sailing on a pirate ship to some desolate island."

"I wouldn't say this is my fault. I'm sure they didn't know I was here."

"Well, don't be so sure about these pirates."

Shamra, who was listening with intense curiosity, looked at Raja with wide eyes. "You're a princess?"

"Yes."

"What's it like to be a princess?"

"Not so nice at the moment," said Raja.

"I think princesses are supposed to be smart," said the younger boy. "How do you expect to get out of this?"

"We will get out of this," said Raja firmly. "All of us. We need to stick together. By the way, what's your name?"

"Yev Confodont."

"Hi, Yev," said Raja. "This is Fedor."

"Hi, Fedor," said Yev.

"And I'm Ivan Sailer," said the older boy.

"Good to meet you," said Raja.

After this first greeting, the group vowed to stick together no matter what. Eventually, the tired captives stopped talking. Raja looked out into the expanse of the sea. Somehow, she had to think of a way to get out of here. She thought about the pirates and how hollow their lives were. She couldn't imagine a life of thievery.

The morning was fully light now. She kept her eyes looking out to the sea, and she eventually saw land in the distance. She assumed it was Kulaly Island.

After sailing for another good while, they reached the island and the anchor was thrown overboard. The five captives were let down in a galley boat with oars and were instructed to row the boat to shore themselves. They did so, and when close enough to land, they stepped into the water and waded to the shore, tugging the boat behind them.

They sat on the shore waiting for what would happen next. Shamra and the two boys were ordered to help take the cargo inland, and Raja and Fedor were instructed to make a fire at the camp. After some time, the pirates came into the camp and sat around the fire roasting fish. Raja thought they ate like famished wolves. She was also thinking they, themselves, weren't much better. She had been starved. Later, they were thankfully allowed to clean up in a nearby stream.

The rest of the day was spent gathering firewood and placing it beside each of the pirate's huts. Raja's back ached by the end of the day. Their last chore was to prepare another meal of fish over the open fire.

When darkness came, the five were separated, and Raja and Fedor were ordered to go into one of the huts. The two walked in, and there, sitting on a chair at a small desk was a woman wearing pirate garb.

"Ye look confused," said the woman.

"I didn't know a woman would dress like that," said Raja.

The woman reached for a black curly hairpiece and put it on. Then she put on a black pirate hat and a red jacket covered with shiny trinket ornaments. She fastened a fake beard around her head and turned to look at Raja with a scowl.

"You? You are the captain?" asked Raja, in complete surprise.

The captain spoke in a low voice, "Aye, I be the captain. Did I have ye scared?"

"Of course."

Laughing in a mocking manner the pirate twirled the curls on her beard. "My disguise brings the fear and respect that I want when I raid ships."

Raja was astounded that a woman could perform such treachery. "How can you, a woman, be a pirate captain?"

The woman took off her hairpiece and beard. "Ah, that's a long story, me mate," she said as she leaned back on her chair.

Raja thought the woman's actions could convincingly be that of a man's, but not absolutely. She could still see her feminine side. It was odd that the woman called her a "mate." She knew it was just an expression, but nonetheless it sounded friendlier than anything else so far.

"Tell me your story," said Raja, genuinely sounding interested.

The pirate woman eyed Raja and then the boy. "What's in yer pouch, lad?" asked the pirate.

"Nothing," said Fedor.

"There be something. Empty it or sleep outside with the snakes."

Fedor slowly took out the doll from his pouch that Raja had given him.

"Give it t' me," said the pirate.

Fedor gave the doll to the pirate. The woman looked at the doll in amusement.

"Odd that a lad would have such a unique and beautiful doll. How did ye get this doll?"

"Raja gave it me."

The pirate looked at Raja.

"Where did this doll come from?"

"A young lord gave it to me."

"A young lord you say. What's his name?"

"Pavel."

"Where did he get it from?" asked the pirate.

"The tzarina."

"Interestin', I think this doll be worth a fair bit of doubloons so now it's mine. Mine t' keep!" The pirate stood up and turned her back to Raja and Fedor. "Ye see, the first step be teachin' ye how to rob." Quickly turning around, the pirate made close eye contact with Fedor and said in a stern voice, "Or perhaps ye already know how."

Fedor was startled.

Raja wanted to scream at the pirate to stop and to give back the doll, but she held her tongue. Somehow, she felt she shouldn't protest the pirate taking the doll. She hoped something good would come of it.

"Who is this lad?"

"He is an orphan and I want to help him."

"Then I be right. He will fit right in."

Raja wanted to say that no, he wouldn't, and it wasn't right.

"What's in yer hair?" asked the captain.

"It's a scarf. My mother gave it to me."

The captain eyed the scarf and felt it with her fingers. "A silk scarf be worth something."

"Please don't take it. It's my only memory of my mother," said Raja, in a pleading tone.

"Under one condition: that ye wear it like a pirate."

"I always wear my scarf," said Raja, as tactfully as she could. "And I will wear it like a pirate."

"Good, ye will fit right in, too."

The captain sat down at her desk again. A crow came and sat on the ledge of the open window, squawked three times, and then did a little dance. The captain took some pieces of fish bone covered with bits of meat and set it on the ledge.

"Me entertainment," said the captain. "Didn't take long to train it. Crows be smart." The crow took the remains of the fish and flew off.

Raja found the incident very amusing and it definitely helped to calm her. "You said you had a long story. Tell it to us."

The pirate seemed to like the request and motioned for Raja and Fedor to sit opposite her, next to the fire.

"Me father was a sailor. He taught me everythin' he knew. I grew up t' be a master sailor, just as good as any man. We passed our time singin' songs o' the sea and learnin' how to read and write. He learned from books given to 'im by people he met on his journeys."

Raja found the captain's past interesting. "So, he was a merchant?"

"Aye, he travelled all over the Land of Rousse. One day, me father was on one o' his trade routes, when pirates robbed him. He was taken away when he didn't surrender. I don't know what happened t' him."

"I'm sorry about your father," said Raja.

The captain thought about her comment. "I missed him terribly. He used t' call me Chamomile."

"That's a pretty name."

"Thanks. And if ye want to know, I call meself Cham."

"What happened to you?"

"I was kidnapped by the pirates and was forced t' become one o' them."

"Are you planning on doing that to us?" asked Raja.

"Time will tell," said the pirate woman, not caring about the fear she inflicted on the two hostages at that precise moment.

Raja fought to control her emotions and continued the conversation. "How did you feel when you were kidnapped?"

"I hated piracy, just like I suspect ye will."

"Do you still hate it now?"

"I became accustomed t' it, and it eventually just became me way o' life."

"But do you still hate it?" asked Raja.

The captain raised her voice. "I am the captain. Am I not? People are afraid o' me. I do as I please."

"But do you really hate it deep inside of you?" Raja asked again, wanting to make a point.

The captain was not expecting her boldness, but liked the intelligent conversation. "Hate it, ye say. Well, I can't say I hate it or don't hate it. I just do it. I plan out the attack and the next one and the next one. It's survival."

"Do you believe that there is any good in this world to be done by you, or do you believe that your life now is all it can be?"

The pirate leaned back in her chair and thought about that question before she answered. "Good? What's good about life? Isn't everyone just tryin' t' get a piece o' bread t' eat?"

"They are, but it's how you do it."

"What about ye? Ye were stolen. Fedor was stolen and the others. That's not good. Where be there good? Everyone's doing the same thing."

"True, there is a lot of wickedness, but one can still find goodness."

"Where?" asked the pirate.

"Goodness is in beauty," said Raja.

"Beauty? What be beauty? I only see misery."

"Beauty comes from doing good."

The pirate sat back and listened with interest. She seemed genuinely intrigued by Raja's comments. "Do ye mean goodness makes beauty?"

"Yes," said Raja, surprised at the captain's understanding. "And evil makes darkness. Everyone has a choice to create beauty or darkness. You have to make a choice to follow good for the sake of yourself and for others. When you give people goodness, you make beauty grow."

The pirate was silent again as if in faraway thought. She said, "How can I make any beauty grow now? I don't even know what beauty be anymore."

"Beauty is love and love is what makes others value life. It is being kind, just, and honest," said Raja, hoping the pirate would understand.

"I've done too much and seen too much. Who would want love from me?"

"If there is forgiveness," said Raja with sincerity in her eyes, "even you can give love."

The pirate put her head into her hands. "No, it's not fer me," said the pirate, with dismay in her voice.

"It can be. I know it would seem impossible for you to change and leave this life, but if you trust, it will come to you. You need to be determined to hate what is wicked and love what is good. Your determination will change you."

The pirate looked up to the ceiling. "Hate what be wicked? Aye, what I do is wicked." The pirate then stared at Raja. "And do I hate it, ye ask?"

"Yes," said Raja. "Deep inside of you, do you hate what you are doing?'

"Raja, ye remind me o' me father's words." And with that last statement, the woman ordered everyone to sleep. Raja and Fedor slept on a pallet, and the pirate captain slept on her own pallet. The night was quiet except for the sound of owls. It reminded Raja of Pavel. She wondered how he was feeling about her disappearance and what he was planning. She had no doubt he would come for her.

Chapter 25

The Boulder

The next few weeks were more or less all the same, working for the pirates, and the two girls and three boys were mostly left alone. There was a lot of time for Raja to think and sometimes anger got the best of her. At the moment, she was picking some wild berries as a midmorning meal. Her thoughts of anger toward her uncle, made her plunk her berries a little too hard into her bowl and juice squirted out.

Her being here was his fault and he certainly did not have a conscience. Why was sitting on the throne so important to him at the expense of other people's lives? Raja wondered if Hannah knew where she was. She seemed to know everything that was going on. If Hannah's father knew he probably didn't care since he already had his coin. Raja sighed. She knew it was no use staying angry. It wouldn't solve anything and besides it made her feel miserable.

A few feet away from her, an older pirate woman was also picking berries. Short in stature, she was having difficulty picking from the taller bushes. She had a cough and didn't look that well to Raja. There were other women on the island as well and Raja thought they were wives. At first, she found it odd that a pirate should have a wife, but pirates were human as well. Everyone needs someone to love, despite what they do with their lives.

Putting aside her feelings of resentment, Raja resolved to use her energy for the good. Walking over to the pirate wife, Raja poured her berries inside the woman's bowl. A look of surprise and gratitude came over the woman's face and she put her stained hands together and smiled. Raja smiled back. She was thankful that a small act of kindness could make a difference in this pirate's wife, but even more thankful for the difference it made in her own life right now. Putting a smile on her own face, made Raja feel a lot better.

Raja went back to picking more berries and thought about the pirate captain. She wondered if their conversation had impacted the captain in any way. She had tried to live out her convictions by thinking of something kind she could do for the captain. She hoped that bringing her wild berries every day and leaving them at her door would be noticed.

Ivan's loud calling interrupted Raja's thoughts. "Raja, come over here."

Ivan, Yev, Shamra, and Fedor were not that far away and were stacking firewood beside a hut.

Raja waved at Ivan and walked toward the group. When she got there, she let everyone eat a share of the berries she had picked.

"Raja, have you thought of a way out of here yet?"

"No, have you?"

"As a matter of fact, I have," said Ivan. "I've been talking about it with Yev for the last few days. He agrees it's a good plan."

"He would," said Shamra. "You are two years older."

"You don't mean we would take the pirates hostage, do you?" asked Fedor with wide eyes.

"No, it's nothing like that. We wouldn't stand a good chance of winning because there are too many of them."

"Trust me," said Yev. "It's a good solid plan."

"And I don't see anyone else offering a solution," said Ivan.

Raja, somewhat surprised at Ivan's initiative, looked around to see if the pirates were watching. "Let's go into the woods and gather more firewood. You can tell us about your plan there."

"All right, follow me," said Ivan. He led them into the thickest part of the woods. They huddled together in a close circle. "Now, here is the plan. I know how to sail a ship."

"Since when do you know how to sail a ship?" asked Raja.

"I worked on ships for two years. I know I could sail it myself. I could tell everyone exactly what to do on the ship. Everyone else can pull the ropes, and I can climb the rigs to adjust the sails," said Ivan.

"How would this work? They would see us taking their ship," said Shamra. "And then think of what would happen to us."

"We could leave at night," said Ivan, trying to sound convincing.

"Don't the pirates keep watch at night?" asked Raja. "I'm sure the captain has someone posted all of the time."

"I've been watching them, and as far as I can see, no one keeps watch," said Ivan. "They all drink and then fall asleep."

Raja wasn't sure it was the greatest idea, but then again, it might work. And she certainly didn't want to stay here. Perhaps this was their way out. “I am assuming this means that we sneak out of our huts during the night and meet somewhere,” she said.

“Precisely,” said Ivan. “We can meet behind that big boulder that is along the shore.”

“Which big boulder?” asked Fedor.

“There is only one,” said Yev.

“Don’t worry,” said Raja as she put her arm around Fedor. “I’m going to be with you.”

Ivan looked around the group to see if everyone was in agreement with his plan. No one protested. “Let’s do it tonight,” said Ivan. The group nodded in agreement.

“And don’t anyone fall asleep,” said Shamra, “or you might be left behind.”

“Let’s get back before we cause suspicion,” said Raja.

The group made their way back to the camp with their arms filled with firewood and continued their work until sunset. That night everyone lay in bed waiting anxiously for the pirates to fall asleep. Raja and Fedor were in one hut, Yev was by himself in another, and Ivan and Shamra were farther down in a different hut.

Raja heard the heavy breathing of the pirate captain. The time seemed right. Slowly, the two of them got up and sneaked out of the hut. The captain didn’t awaken. They ran to the boulder as fast as they could.

When they got there, Shamra and Ivan were already there. They waited for another good while.

“Do you think something has happened?” asked Shamra.

“Let’s hope not,” said Raja.

“I see the moon is on our side tonight – full and bright,” said Ivan.

Raja looked at the moon. "A sure help, but not if we have to wait for Yev all night."

"Should we keep waiting for him or leave him behind?" asked Shamra.

"You said yourself for no one to fall asleep or they would be left behind," said Raja.

"I know I said it, but easier said than done. Don't you agree?"

"Yes, I do agree. I just hope nothing bad has happened."

"I see him," said Ivan. "He's coming."

Everyone sighed in relief. When Yev got to the boulder he was out of breath and spoke between gasps of air. "My pirate wouldn't stop talking. He kept on telling me stories about piracy and their scare tactics, good ones too."

"What are you talking about?" asked Shamra. "They're awful."

"No, they're not. They're interesting."

Ivan turned to Yev, indicating for him to not talk so loud. "Come on. Let's get to the ship before we're found out," said Ivan. They ran down to the water and climbed aboard one of the galley boats. They steadily rowed to the pirate ship.

Once aboard the ship, Ivan began explaining what needed to be done. They all worked furiously to get the sails up. Ivan walked along the yards and adjusted the sails.

When Ivan gave the signal, the anchor was taken up and the ship was set sailing. They each took turns climbing to the crow's nest to keep watch, and as far as they could see, no one was coming after them.

Yev was at the wheel. Everyone wanted a turn at the wheel.

"Ahoy," said Yev. "Raise the jolly roger. Fire in the hole!"

"What? Are you now a pirate?" asked Raja.

"It would be some fun, wouldn't it?" said Yev, as he played with the wheel and shouted pirate talk. "Sail ho, load the six pounders!"

"What nonsense," said Raja.

"It's my turn next," said Fedor.

"Then mine," said Shamra.

Raja admitted to herself it did feel exciting to sail a pirate ship, but more than that she felt a sense of relief. They were actually getting away from that dreadful island, and in no time, they would be safe again in Kazan. Well, perhaps not safe, but safer than this situation anyway.

Then suddenly, a growly voice boomed in the darkness.

"Aaaarrrrgggghhhh! Who's sailin' me ship?" A pirate appeared from the shadows. "Shiver me timbers!" he shouted. "Tryin' t' escape are ye all?"

Raja and the others were surprised and frightened.

"Ye better turn this ship around right now if ye don't want a finger or two gone."

Raja grabbed Fedor, and Shamra grabbed Yev's hand. Yev shook Shamra's hand off. "I can handle this," he said.

The group slowly backed away. The pirate waved his cutlass at them.

"So ye thought ye could escape did ye?" The pirate laughed. "Well, we pirates be always one step ahead. Ye woke me from me sleep with all yer loud hollerin'. Not sure what I'm goin' t' do about that."

Raja shouted out bravely. "Why don't you let the captain decide?"

"The captain's not here right now. So I be yer captain."

"But the captain won't like it if she's not informed first. You might get in trouble with her, and I don't think that would be a good thing for you."

The pirate took Raja's comment into consideration. "Yer got some thinkin' there. We'll just wait fer the captain, but ye might be sorry."

Relieved Raja whispered into Fedor's ear. "It's okay. I don't think the captain is that mean."

Disappointment fell on the captive group as they journeyed back to the island. The pirate ordered them to get off the ship and row to shore. Once they were on land they were taken to the large boulder on the shore and their hands were tied.

Not too much later, they stood with their backs turned to the captain, who arrogantly leaned against the large boulder. Surprisingly, the captain was calm, as if she had been expecting the escape.

"No one has ever escaped this island. And no one has ever tried a second time. In other words, after people get lashed the first time, they don't want a second lashin'. I call this me lashin' boulder. Do ye understand?" asked the captain.

Their bodies starting to tremble, the five captives quickly nodded.

"Hand me the whip," said the captain who then walked to stand behind the children. The pirate gave the whip to the captain, and she immediately cracked it in the air. Screams and cries came from the escapees. "How many lashes should it be?" asked the captain, looking at the pirate.

"For stealin' a ship, five each," said the pirate.

"Five it be!" shouted the captain. "Kneel!" The group kneeled down, all crying and trembling in terror. "Strike one!" said the captain as she raised her whip.

"Stop," cried Raja, "we won't do it again."

"That ain't good enough!"

Desperately trying to think of something, Raja gritted her teeth with a grimaced face, expecting the first lash. "Isn't coin more important than your lashes?" she shouted.

The captain twirled her whip in the air. "Speak yer mind before me lay the first lash!"

"What worth is a princess with scars?"

"Ah! Ye speak like ye 'ave some intelligence left in that tremblin' brain o' yers. I can save ye, but ye will watch the others suffer!"

"No!" screamed Raja who thought the situation just got worse than before. "Pavel will reward you for leaving them unharmed!"

"Ye speak like he's comin'! Rest assured, he will never find ye!"

"You can take us back to Kazan. If you give us all up, you will be doubly rewarded."

"I reckon ye mean hung instead, for all me bad deeds as a pirate!"

Raja could understand the captain's fear. "No, my mother would not do that!"

"Once a pirate, always a pirate!"

"You can change!"

"Enough! That ain't in me plans!"

Raja's body broke out into a sweat. She had to think of something else. "If you leave the others unharmed you can get more for all of us!"

A loud crack of the whip sounded in the air.

"If it weren't fer yer quick thinking and me love o' coin yer backs would 'ave met me whip instead of the air."

"We are grateful!" said Raja. "Please let us go!"

"But, me needs to hear that ye will never try to escape again!"

"You can have our word!" said Raja.

"That's not good enough!"

"We will never try to escape again!" yelled Raja.

"Do ye mean NEVER!"

"NEVER! NEVER!" they all yelled.

The captain brought down her whip. Raja's eyes filled with tears as she released her stress. The captain yelled at the pirate. "Untie them!"

"But shouldn't they have some punishment?" asked the other pirate.

"No! No!" shouted the captives.

"Hold your tongue and let me think or I'll whip you anyways!"

Fedor cried louder than before.

"Hold your tongue!" shouted the captain.

"Fedor, close your mouth or you'll get us into trouble again!" shouted Yev.

Trying to obey the command, Fedor tried to be as quiet as he could, but little squeaky noises still escaped his mouth.

The captain walked back and forth behind the children, acting as if she were in deep thought and then finally stopped and raised her whip straight up in the air. "Ye will all be chained to yer beds at night from now on." She cracked her whip in the air. "Do ye understand?"

"Yes! Yes!" said the captives.

"Untie them!" shouted the captain. The pirate obeyed the command.

It felt like an eternity before the ropes fell from Raja's wrists. She rubbed her sore skin, but it was nothing compared to what could have happened. Their punishment was mild compared to what others had no doubt suffered.

Her suggestion of being worth more without scars seemed to have changed the captain's mind, but Raja wondered if the captain really would have lashed them. Surely she knew any of them were worth more unscarred. The captain's threats could have been just a scare tactic. But the thought of being exchanged for coin repulsed her. It would surely be the end of her freedom, as she knew it and she would never get back to Kazan.

Perhaps becoming a pirate would eventually be their way of escape. But the idea of doing what pirates did seemed just as bad. She couldn't imagine any of them becoming a pirate. She contemplated the idea as she put her arms around Fedor to comfort him. She and Fedor led the group away from the boulder to sit on the sand of the shore. She would have a lot to think about.

Looking back from where they had just stood with tied hands, Raja looked at the rock. She wouldn't remember it for the bad that had just happened. Instead she saw it as a place of salvation. She listened to the small voice that spoke to her soul. The rock was her father – strong and protective – unchanging. He wouldn't let her down.

Chapter 26

No Choice

"What other choice do we have?" asked Raja, as she threw more wood on the fire to build up the flame for their evening meal. The five of them were cooking their own meal tonight and were separate from the pirates, but could still hear them laughing.

The pirates were taking turns jumping over the fire. After staring at them for a moment Raja continued. "All the pirate captain wants is her ransom coin, but the tzarina may not find us before the Dracians do. I think becoming a pirate is the best plan for an escape. I'm sure I can convince the pirate captain to keep us."

"I don't know if I could bear becoming a pirate," said Shamra. "I have never stolen anything in my life, and now to make a life of it is more than I can stand."

Raja turned the fish onto its other side. "You are not making a life of it. It is only until we can find a way to escape."

"But I wouldn't know how to like being a pirate," said Shamra.

Yev smiled and thrust his chest forward. "Leave it to me. I will show you how to be a pirate. The idea sounds exciting."

"I don't mean to really like it," said Raja. "Get your head on your shoulders."

"Well, if I have to do it, I might as well like it in the meantime."

Raja looked disgusted. She looked up to see if they were being watched. Today the pirates sat in their own groups, cooking their own meals.

"Ivan, what do you think of the idea?" asked Raja.

"I think it's a good idea. We aren't going to be able to steal a ship again after we were caught."

"Do you think they somehow knew we were going to take the ship?" asked Raja.

"I don't know," said Ivan, "but it seems suspicious that a pirate was onboard."

Raja looked at Shamra and continued her conversation. "The other concern is that we could all be sold into slavery, and then escape would be next to impossible. So, if we can convince the pirates that we would be useful to them, they would probably keep us. Do you think you could do it, Shamra?"

"I'll do what I have to," she said.

Shamra, who was sitting next to Raja, got up and went to sit a little farther away. She motioned Raja to follow her. Raja left the boys by themselves and followed Shamra.

"Something strange is happening to Yev," said Shamra.

"I think I've noticed," said Raja.

"He's not being chained up at night anymore. He sits with the pirates in the hut and listens to their stories. And the concerning thing is that Yev is enjoying them."

"I wonder if it was him who leaked the information that we were stealing the ship," said Raja.

"You might be right. The pirates would have a way of getting it out of Yev."

"He'll come back to his senses," said Raja, hoping she was right. "He's just being a boy."

The pirates were laughing loudly tonight. One of them yelled over to the group. "Yev, come over here. Yer goin' t' like this one!"

Yev obediently got up and went over to the group of pirates. One of the pirates got up. He began telling a story while moving his arms wildly about and kicking up his legs multiple times. His face twisted with a menacing expression.

Yev was captivated, and every time the story came to a scary part, Yev was encouraged to join in. He had the pirates roaring with laughter with his uninhibited antics.

Raja was worried about Yev. He seemed to be enjoying himself way too much. She was glad Fedor was not being drawn into the pirates' talk. Thankfully Ivan wasn't listening to the pirates like Yev, but then again, they would all have to change if they were going to pretend to be pirates. That chore certainly wasn't welcome to Raja. But on further thought, she decided that now was as good a time as any.

"Come on," said Raja, "let's join them. We have to start sometime, and the sooner we do, the better." Raja asked Ivan and Fedor to come with them as well. The friends followed Raja and they sat by the pirates around the fire.

"Well blimey, look who came over," said one of the pirates.

"We want to become pirates," said Ivan.

"That didn't take long," said the pirate. "Yer makin' a good choice. It's nothin' but t' best."

"Why's that?" asked Ivan.

"'Cause all ye need t' do is sit in one o' those ships and look out at the horizon. Sooner or later ye spot a ship, and yer work's half done."

"How do you capture the ship?"

"We use scare tactics, and which one we use be decided by the captain."

Raja looked around for the captain. She was absent from the group.

"What are the scare tactics?" asked Ivan.

"One way t' approach the merchant ship be with a false flag, and pretend we be in trouble."

"So you lure them to your ship?" asked Ivan.

"Aye. When they come over t' help us and be in close enough, we scare t' life out o' them by puttin' up our flag."

"Their flag means 'surrender or die,'" said Yev, proud that he knew that information. Raja gave him a puzzled look. Yev ignored the look and continued enthusiastically. "The captain shoots a cannon ball right in front of the ship. The crew gets so frightened that the pirates can board the ship without any problem and take the cargo. And sometimes they get a big fortune."

"Is that what you want Yev, a fortune?" Ivan caught himself saying the wrong thing. "I mean, ah, good Yev, that sounds great. A fortune is always what I wanted."

"What if the crew doesn't want to surrender?" asked Raja.

"If they don't want t' surrender, we use force. We batter their ship, and if that don't work we take down the crew."

Raja felt light-headed.

At that moment, Yev spoke up again.

"What about the other tactic you told me about, standing on the side of the ship with everyone yelling and waving their weapons."

"Blimey, I forgot that. Jolly point, Yev," said the pirate. "We yell threats and look as mean and ugly as we can. We wave our weapons in the air, threatenin' death if they don't surrender. That usually works extra well, with no take-downs."

"So what happens after the ship surrenders?" asked Ivan.

"We climb aboard and take hostages. Any resistors, we take them down. It's all done as smartly as that. We don't like t' take people down, but if they resist we have t'. We aim t' get the captain o' the ship as smartly as possible." At that moment, the pirate stood up with his hands around his neck and yelled, "And put a rope around his neck!"

The pirate looked scary, and it was at this point that Raja was second-guessing herself. Could she really do it and fake being a pirate? She wasn't sure. She couldn't imagine killing anyone or even witnessing it.

But she had to go through with this. What other way was there? She was sure she wouldn't be expected to take anyone down anyway. She could stay in the pirate ship. But of course, then she would be expected to load cannons or shoot or do something like that. Could she do that? Raja shook those thoughts from her mind. There just wasn't any other choice.

She would talk to the captain tomorrow and boldly tell her that they were all surrendering and would become pirates. That was just the way it had to be. Then she would secretly plan their escape.

Raja felt light-headed.

At that moment, Yev spoke up again.

"What about the other tactic you told me about, standing on the side of the ship with everyone yelling and waving their weapons."

"Blimey, I forgot that. Jolly point, Yev," said the pirate. "We yell threats and look as mean and ugly as we can. We wave our weapons in the air, threatenin' death if they don't surrender. That usually works extra well, with no take-downs."

"So what happens after the ship surrenders?" asked Ivan.

"We climb aboard and take hostages. Any resistors, we take them down. It's all done as smoothly as that. We don't like to take people down, but other pirates we have. We aim to get the captain o' the ship as smartly as possible." At that moment, the pirate stood up with his hands around his neck and called, "And put a rope around his neck!"

The pirate looked [illegible] at this point that Raja was secretly questioning herself. Could she really do it and take being a pirate? She wasn't sure. She couldn't imagine sitting around the [illegible] interesting it.

But she had to go through with this. What other way was there? She was sure she wouldn't be expected to take anyone down anyway. She could stay in the pirate ship. But of course, then she would be expected to load cannons or scout or do something like that. Could she do that? Raja shook these thoughts from her mind; there just wasn't any other choice.

She would talk to the captain tomorrow and boldly tell her that they were all surrendering and would become pirates. That was just the way it had to be. Then she would secretly plan their escape.

Chapter 27

Fedor's Sling and Stone

"How do ye expect me t' believe that?" asked the pirate captain, who was sitting at her desk in the hut.

"You can have my word on it," said Raja, who sat alone with the captain and was trying very hard to convince her that she was being truthful.

"Do ye mean t' tell me that ye be takin' back everythin' ye told me on yer first day here? Ye nearly had me convinced t' change me life."

"Well, I can change my mind, can't I?"

"Somehow, I just don't think ye really want t' be a pirate. Ye are up t' somethin."

This conversation wasn't going as Raja expected. She had to think of a quick alibi. "I will prove to you that I will make a good pirate," said Raja.

"I couldn't think o' anythin' meself," said the captain with sarcasm.

"Give me a cutlass," said Raja.

The captain looked at Raja with amusement. "So ye know how t' fight with a cutlass, do ye?"

"Try me," said Raja.

"Yo ho," said the humored captain and handed Raja one of her weapons that were held inside her sash.

They stepped outside, and Raja took her stance. The weapons clashed. Raja stepped back and then forward. The cutlass operated differently from the swords she was used to.

With her own cutlass ready to strike, the captain eyed Raja. "I see ye be quite skillful."

The fighting continued. "But why would I keep ye if I can get a good ransom for ye?" asked the captain.

"I'll be worth more to you as a pirate," said Raja and hit hard with her cutlass. "My skills will add double to your crew! You will never lose a raid with me onboard."

Hitting hard again, Raja knocked the cutlass from the captain's hand.

Quickly picking up her weapon, the captain growled, being annoyed that she had been caught off-guard, allowing Raja to make a superior play. It was clear that she had underestimated Raja's strength and skill. The captain lunged at Raja and returned three harder blows to Raja's blade.

The fight continued for a few more seconds, and the cutlass was knocked from Raja's hand. The pirate had the curved edge of her blade to Raja's throat. "Ye be good, but it's not convincin' that ye really want to become a pirate."

The captain let Raja go. The princess was breathing heavily and knew she was out of practice.

"Avast!" said the captain. "Look who we have comin."

Raja looked out into the sea and saw a ship approaching over the horizon. "What ship is it?" she asked.

Before speaking, the captain waited a few minutes for the ship to come closer. "It's the Dracians. I can tell by the lion carving on one of their small boats. They have a white flag meanin' they come in peace."

Raja could see the two flags on top of the ship. Yes, one flag was white and the other flag was striped blue and white with a black diamond in the center. It had three horizontal stripes with a larger white strip in the middle.

The captain ordered Raja to stay where she was, and then she left to notify the other pirates. In short order, Shamra, Fedor, and Ivan were sitting with her, but not Yev.

The ship was now much closer and held its position with the anchor. A boat was let down into the water, and several men were rowing to shore.

"Who are they?" asked Shamra.

"The Dracians," said Raja.

"Looks like they are coming for you," said Ivan. "I think Captain Mossovince informed them of your whereabouts."

"This is what the pirate captain was waiting for," said Raja.

"Do you mean ransom coin?" asked Ivan.

"Yes, that's exactly what I mean."

"What about us?" asked Shamra, suddenly feeling very anxious about the situation.

Fedor hung onto Raja. "Don't leave," said Fedor. "I'm scared."

"Don't worry, Fedor. I won't leave you behind," said Raja. She didn't know whether to feel surprised or not. After all, the captain hadn't shown any interest in them, and getting ransom coin was the captain's specialty. Raja was sure she would be delighted with it.

The dilemma as it stood appeared to be the same as when she was first captured. However, there was a new twist to the events, namely, her newly-acquired friends. She couldn't possibly leave them behind.

The men in the boat were now within hearing distance.

"We've got coin!" shouted one of the men.

"How much?" yelled the pirate captain.

"Show us the princess!" they shouted.

The captain ordered one of the pirates to bring Raja down to the shoreline. Standing on the sand with bare feet, Raja stood looking out at the boat and then looked back at her friends. The wind blew against her pretty face and slightly lifted her dress, which was now ragged. She suddenly felt very alone. But she wasn't fearful anymore, instead she felt enraged. Anger settled inside of her at the thought of how this could happen to another human being, and all just for the greed of silver coins.

"Ten hundred silver coins!" shouted the man from the boat.

"Wait!" yelled Raja. She turned to where the captain was standing. "I can't leave without my friends. Ask them for double, and they can also take the others."

The captain walked down to the shore. Her baggy pants flapped in the wind. She always wore a white man's shirt with a black vest and white sash tied around her hips. Her black hair was naturally curly and hung just past her shoulders. It was the masculine look she needed to maintain her authority.

Facing Raja, the captain stood with her legs apart and hands on her hips. Her face was hard but her eyes looked sad. The pirate's conflicting emotions made Raja believe there was still sympathy inside her heart. At that moment, the captain's crow flew down and sat on her shoulder. Giving her crow a few pets, the captain thought the offer over. She finally said, "I was expectin' this from you. The Dracian is lowballin' me anyway. And I like ye, so for ye I will do it."

The pirate shouted back to the Dracians. "Give me double, and ye can have four more—a lass and three lads!"

The men in the boat talked between themselves for a minute. "Agreed," they said.

Then suddenly, there was loud yelling from the pirates along the shore, and a young voice called out. "I'm not going! I'm a pirate now, and that's what I want to be—a pirate!"

The voice was Yev's. The pirates cheered. Raja's heart sank. She tried pleading with Yev to come.

"Yev, you're not thinking! Come with us!"

"Why should I? I don't want to be a slave. Here, I can have my freedom."

Ivan stepped forward. It seemed that Yev was telling the truth. He really did want to stay and be a pirate. Ivan couldn't bear the thought of leaving his young friend.

"If Yev is staying, then I want to as well!" yelled Ivan.

"Why should I keep ye?" shouted the captain.

"I'm a good strong sailor, and I know the sea."

The captain was silent for a moment and then said, "Okay, ye can stay, but under one condition, that ye be as fearless as we are."

"You won't be disappointed," said Ivan.

The captain turned her attention toward the men in the boat.

"The two older boys are stayin', but the offer remains. Double, and you can have the other lass and the young lad."

"A deal!" yelled the men.

Momentary relief swept over Raja. At least Shamra and Fedor would be coming with her, but how long they would be together remained to be seen. Raja would do everything she could to keep the three of them united. She ran back to Shamra, and the two of them hugged.

"Am I coming?" asked Fedor.

"Yes," said Raja, "I told you I wouldn't leave you."

"I want to get the sling I made," said Fedor.

"Where is it?" asked Raja at the very same moment the captain approached them.

"It's in the hut," said the captain. "Come with me, Fedor, and I will give it t' ye."

As the captain walked past Raja, she stopped and looked into her face. Raja detected a glimmer of pain in her eyes.

"I forgive you," said Raja.

The captain bent her head and continued into the hut with Fedor. Raja watched her enter the hut and vowed to herself to pray for the pirate captain. It was easy to see that the captain was unhappy with her life, and Raja hoped that one day the pirate would put the past resentments behind her and move toward living a different life.

Moments later, Raja and Shamra were taken and forced to wade through the water to the rowboat with the lion head. The men were ready to row back to their ship and dipped their oars into the water.

"Wait," said Raja with a pleading voice. "Please don't leave without Fedor."

The men halted.

To Raja and Shamra's relief, Fedor finally came from the hut. He ran down to the shore and waded to the boat. He hoisted himself into the boat and the three Dracian captives were on their way to a new destination. The unknown was waiting for them in Dracon. Fedor hung onto his sling that the captain had helped him make. In his hand he rolled the round stone that she had found for him. It was the one nice thing the captain had done for him.

into the boat and the three Dracian captives were on their way to a new destination. The unknown was waiting for them in Dracona. Eadec [illegible] onto his sling that the captain had helped him make. In his hand he rolled the round stone that she had found for him. It was the one nice thing the captain had done for him.

Chapter 28

Dracian Headpiece

Raja, Shamra, and Fedor had arrived in Dracon and were now bowing before the Khan Temujunfar.

"Get up," he said. "I see my princess has finally arrived at the Dragomir Palace. I have been waiting some time for you, and your red hair and fair skin are as lovely as it was said."

Raja felt nauseated.

"Who are these other two?" asked the khan.

"She is my maid-in-waiting, and the younger is my errand boy," said Raja.

The khan looked at Shamra's attire.

"Why is she wearing clothes like a peasant?"

"Her dress was ruined, and the clothes were given to her by a pirate wife."

"I see, but she looks too young to be your maid," said the khan.

"On the contrary, she only looks young for her age."

"How old is she?"

"Sixteen."

The answers seemed to satisfy the khan.

"Do you know your purpose here?" asked the khan.

"No," said Raja.

"Then let me inform you. I have brought you here to become part of our nobility, and to marry the crown prince."

Raja thought she would rather die.

"Do not look so disappointed. You will have more than anyone else in the kingdom, and you will be treated with honor and respect. What more could you ask for?"

"Release me back to Zurkia, so that I may marry for love."

"That is foolishness. You will only be recaptured. Now that you are here, you will marry of my choice. You will have to fulfill your duties as crown princess, and if you fail I will send you back to the pirates."

Raja hoped she could somehow escape before she was forced to fulfill any marital duties, but she answered as the khan expected. "Of course, Khan, I will do everything that is required of me."

"I can already see you will make a good wife. And you shall be given a new name. You will now be referred to as Princess Diamonique."

It was a very beautiful name, but much too long for Raja's liking. She would still call herself Raja when she was not around the khan.

The khan clapped his hands, and the three were taken away. They were led outside by escorts and taken to a different part of the Dragomir Palace. Raja couldn't help but notice the beautifully sculptured building. The rounded palace tops had vivid colors and interesting patterns, so different from Kazan. She walked past a number of very large lion statues. She was glad they were not alive. She noticed pink birds perched on top of several lion heads. They were cockatoos, a bird Kuzma had told her about in one of his stories. It was a very interesting bird she thought, with its crown of red, yellow, and white feathers. Both girls were surprised when the bird greeted them with a few words.

When they were led inside the palace again, Fedor was taken to a different part of the building, and Raja and Shamra were led into a room laden with silk materials, artwork, and exotic furniture. There they were given everything they needed and were allowed to rest.

"I'm glad they allowed us to stay together," said Shamra.

"Me, too. I'm surprised he believed you were sixteen," said Raja smiling.

"Well, I do have a mature look, don't you think?"

Raja looked her over with one eye. "Sort of," she said.

"Are you trying to be funny?" asked Shamra.

"A little," said Raja with a tilted head.

"I guess we need humor right now," said Shamra. "I hope Fedor will be okay."

"Don't worry. When I become princess as they say, I will demand to see him. Remember—from now on you are my maid-in-waiting and you are born of a knight and upper-class lady."

"Okay," said Shamra.

Raja and Shamra were exhausted and fell asleep almost immediately. When they awoke servants were waiting to serve them food. They were extremely glad to have something to eat.

Raja couldn't help but think what a contrast this was to the life they had just experienced on Kulaly Island. Their diet had consisted mostly of fish and a few vegetables. Here, there was every kind of food conceivable. She didn't know what most of it was. She and Shamra cautiously tasted all the new foods. Raja thought most of it was delicious.

The next few weeks for Raja were spent learning the new culture and teaching Shamra how to be a lady-in-waiting. She admitted that they were being treated extremely well. As far as their needs went, nothing could have been better.

She also saw that there was no way of escape. Other servants and escorts were constantly around them. She even had seen the bailiff that used to work at the manor. She was sure he had looked her way and given her a haughty look. It appeared he was a spy after all. She knew she would have to be very careful with whatever she did to get herself out of Baku.

Shamra came into Raja's room and helped her with her dress and hair.

"Raja," said Shamra, "I've been informed that you are to meet the crown prince tomorrow."

"Tomorrow!" said Raja. "Shamra, what's going to happen? Am I really going to marry him?"

"I don't know, but I should think it would be better than being a pirate."

Raja agreed with that, but hoped it wouldn't happen. She dreadfully missed the manor and everyone there.

The next day came too soon. There was a flurry of maids doting over her. Two of the maids were twins and looked so much alike, Raja couldn't tell them apart. She thought they were a bit younger than she was, and surprisingly they had hair like Shamra's. Their eyes were exquisite looking with very unusual color.

Raja rather liked the girls, as they were jolly and fun to be with. They let her choose between two dresses. One was a brightly-colored dress covered in silk and trimmed with fur and beads, and the other was a flamboyant hooped dress, with symmetrical designs and jewels. She chose the one trimmed with fur.

The maids did not allow her to wear her scarf. Instead, they asked her to choose one of the headpieces that now belonged to her. They were all so very extravagant. She finally chose one with green, orange, and purple gems, which were placed around the cap of the headpiece with a green gem in the center.

The headpiece was positioned on her head. The cap was weighted with numerous strands of coral and turquoise beads coming down on her forehead and along her face and then extending past her shoulders. The top of the cap was further covered in beading of all colors and extended upward in the shape of a crown. Her hair was divided and plaited on each side with strands of pearls wrapped around each plait. Silver bells were attached on the ends of her hair.

Her face was carefully painted with makeup, especially around her eyes and on her cheeks. She definitely didn't look like the same girl. Shamra didn't know whether to laugh or cry when she saw her, but decided on laughing.

"Stop laughing," said Raja. "It will give you away. Ladies-in-waiting don't do that."

"Okay, I will save it for later. But I don't know how you can hold your head up with that headpiece full of beads and jewels."

"Yes, it feels awkward and heavy."

"I'm sorry, but your headpiece reminds me of a cockatoo."

"Well then, I'll take that as a compliment because I like cockatoos."

Shamra giggled. "And it's a good thing you have good balance."

"Thanks for that encouragement," said Raja, with some sarcasm in her voice. Raja could see that the servants were waiting for her. She whispered to Shamra. "I feel nervous, but I don't know why. I am definitely not marrying him."

"They will force you to," said Shamra. "Hopefully, he will be a kind person."

Raja gave Shamra a look between despair and hopefulness. Her emotions were in disarray. She remembered her training as a jouster and determined to stay focused. Raja finally indicated that she was ready and was escorted to the waiting crown prince. She walked as gracefully as she could, wearing the Dracian princess headpiece.

Chapter 29

Jafar

Raja and the crown prince sat opposite each other in the barrel-vaulted room. Their table was next to a large window over-looking the village. Tea and various cakes were set out for them to eat.

"What's your name?" asked the crown prince.

Raja was glad to see that he looked about the same age as what she was. She felt she could be herself around him and answered informally.

"Raja."

"Nice name."

"Thank you. Your father wants my name changed to Diamonique, but please call me Raja when we are not in his presence."

"Yes, of course."

"What's your name?"

"Jafar."

"Four of the same letters as in my name."

Jafar smiled, seeming to like the comment.

Raja looked at the sweets on the table. "What is this?" she asked.

"It's baklava. Try it. It has nuts, honey, and cinnamon."

"What's cinnamon?"

"A brown spice. I'm sure you will like it."

Raja bit into the baklava. It was delicious. "May I have another?" she asked.

"Certainly." Jafar handed the plate of sweets to Raja.

He was handsome, she thought, with his dark complexion. And his smile was intriguing. Better to have someone attractive sitting across from her than not.

Raja sipped some tea, as did Jafar. She thought the tea tasted good.

"What do you like doing?" asked Jafar.

"Sword fighting," said Raja.

"Sword fighting! I didn't expect that. You're joking though, aren't you?"

"No, I'm not."

"Well, I will have to entertain you with that then, won't I?"

"I would be delighted."

Raja took another piece of baklava. "What do you like doing?" she asked.

"Falconry."

"Tell me about it."

"I use falcons to hunt quarry."

"I see," said Raja. "How many do you have?"

"Four."

"May I see them?"

"Of course." Jafar led Raja to another part of the palace to see his falcons. He talked to her along the way. "Surely you must like something other than sword fighting."

"I do. I like a lot of things."

"Such as?"

"Horseback riding."

"Well, we make the perfect team then. Would you come with me on a hunting trip with my falcons? I have a grand horse waiting for you."

Raja considered the suggestion and agreed. She missed riding.

Jafar led Raja into a large aviary. The falcons were fascinating. Raja was impressed with the way Jafar handled them. They perched on his leather-protected arms, two on each arm.

"How do you train them?" asked Raja.

"With a lot of patience. I will sit a raptor, which is a young falcon, on my arm for hours to get the bird used to me. I also feed the bird while it is sitting on my arm. That way, it associates me with the food."

"I see," said Raja, "and so when you let the bird go, it will follow you because it knows you provide food for it."

"Yes," said Jafar, "that's right."

"Do the falcons come back to you when you let them go?"

"No, not always. Sometimes I am not close enough to lure them back when they catch their quarry. When that happens, they will eat their quarry and decide to stay in the wild."

"How do you catch new falcons?"

"I trap them, but only take raptors, or I take a chick from a nest."

"Isn't that cruel?" asked Raja.

"Not really, because the other chicks have a better chance of survival. I always let my falcons go free after I have had them for a season. I don't keep them forever."

"Makes sense," said Raja.

"Come with me to see your horse," said Jafar.

"I'd love to," said Raja who felt honored that she would already own a horse. Jafar led Raja to a stable with one of the most beautiful horses she had ever seen, pure white with a black mane and tail. She desperately wanted to ride again.

"It's gorgeous."

"She is and very well-trained. I know you will like her."

"Where's your horse?"

"Down here."

They walked down to another stall.

"Oh, pure black, except for a white mane and tail," said Raja.

"The horses will make a good spectacle riding together," said Jafar. Raja wondered where else they would ride besides on their hunting trip. "It's tradition for a couple to ride through the streets of Baku."

A couple, thought Raja. Jafar seemed kind, but this was not what she wanted. But in the end she realized she might not have any other choice. Jafar escorted Raja back to their table. They sat and talked for a while longer and then parted ways.

The next day, the falconry outing went as planned, and Raja admitted it had been fun. She did love her horse. Jafar was also fun to be with. He continued to take her on country rides with their horses. They talked about a lot of things, and Raja told stories of what it was like where she came from. She enjoyed his company.

Jafar also spent time teaching her how to use the bow and arrow, something she had not learned to do yet. Admittedly, she enjoyed the sport and caught on very well. As time went on, Jafar had a difficult time winning the matches. In fact, they were about even a lot of the times.

Shamra was turning out to be an excellent lady-in-waiting and seemed to enjoy the work. She fixed Raja's hair and tied the sashes around her dress in unique knots. There were so many choices of different dresses to wear that most of the time Raja just let Shamra choose.

Today, Shamra chose a very brightly-colored orange, purple, and yellow robe with geometric designs. To match the robe, Raja wore poofy orange pants that were wrapped at the ankle. She then slipped into some stylish shoes that were curled at the tips.

"That looks gorgeous on you," said Shamra.

"Thank you. I like it as well."

"Do you like him?" asked Shamra.

"Do you mean Jafar?"

"Yes."

Raja smiled rather sweetly. "I do like him."

"Is that just a friend-type of like or something more?" asked Shamra with raised eyebrows.

"Oh, it's just a friend-type of like."

"Are you sure?"

Raja wasn't so sure. Maybe she did like him as more than just a friend. She certainly liked being with him. "To be honest, I don't know. He has turned out to be very kind and generous. And we have so much fun together when we practice our sports. But I admit that I miss Pavel. I don't know what the right thing to do is. Somehow I feel torn in two," said Raja. "And my mind doesn't have any rest."

"Raja," said Shamra. "It's okay. We don't know if we will ever return to Zurkia. You are fortunate Jafar is a kind young man, since you are being forced to marry him. You can start a new life here."

Raja thought about what Shamra was saying. "Yes, I can see your point of view."

"Then be determined to accept that this is how it is now. Quit fighting the situation in your mind or you will become exhausted."

"Perhaps you are right."

"I know I am right. It is better to be agreeable than to resist the khan. Resistance would only make it more difficult for everyone," said Shamra.

"That's true."

Shamra smiled at Raja. "You'll make a beautiful bride. I'm sure you will be happy with Jafar."

Raja wanted to believe that she would be happy, but somehow, even though what Shamra said made a lot of sense, the whole situation still made her feel uneasy. But, despite her feelings, Raja knew Shamra was right. She would simply have to go on without her family and friends, and even Pavel. She certainly didn't want to start any wars in the Land of Rousse. She agreed it was better to do it the khan's way and to accept the fact that she would not sit on Zurkia's throne. Perhaps some day in the future she would still meet her tzarina mother.

Feeling satisfied with her conclusions, Raja asked about Fedor. "I have been asking for Fedor, but every time I ask, I am turned down."

"I'll look into that," said Shamra. "I'll get him to come see you as soon as possible."

“Thanks,” said Raja. “I really appreciate that. I just want to know that he is doing okay.”

“It’s no trouble,” said Shamra.

Chapter 30

Fedor's Secret

Jafar was waiting for Raja in the spacious courtyard when she arrived. The courtyard was designed with wide stairs and a long row of large white pillars that extended the length of the open area. The space was decorated with numerous pots of yellow zinnia flowers.

Raja had definitely succeeded in captivating Jafar's attention with all the time she had spent with him since she had arrived at Dragomir Palace. And if she was honest she had enjoyed the time as well. She had been anticipating the duel and now stood before Jafar with her heart beating a little faster than usual.

"You look beautiful even when you carry a sword," he said.

"Why wouldn't I?"

"It isn't exactly lady-like is it?"

"It is if I say it is."

"Ah, I detect a little spirit."

"And there's a great deal more."

"I'm looking forward to it," said Jafar.

"On guard!" she said.

The two were drawn into their sword fight, once again not expecting their opponent's skill.

"You surprise me today," said Jafar.

"I take that as a compliment."

"Indeed it is."

Neither one was seeking to end the sword fight, but instead kept on with their display of skillful moves. Jafar forced Raja up the stairs. She did not have much experience fighting on stairs, so Jafar gained on her and quickly locked his sword with hers.

Jafar moved close to Raja's face. "Marry me," he said.

"Do I have a choice?"

Raja pushed Jafar away with her knee. He did a back flip down the stairs. Then as quickly as pattering rain, Raja stepped down the stairs. She clashed her sword with his, the both of them criss-crossing blades at a tremendous speed. Jafar backed her toward a pillar. He locked her sword again.

"Say that you want to," said Jafar.

"I wouldn't say this is the time and place."

"What better time than this? You mesmerize me."

"What about love?"

Jafar looked into her eyes. "I love you," he whispered.

Raja ducked and shot away. The two continued fighting, not letting on that they were tired. Raja knocked the sword from Jafar's hand and had him at a standstill.

"What is love?" said Raja.

"Beauty," he said.

Raja wanted to believe him.

"I won," she said. Raja turned and was about to leave.

"Wait," called Jafar. He bent down on one knee in front of her and looked up into her face. "Will you marry me?"

Raja didn't want to say no, and she didn't want to say yes. But she decided the marriage would happen anyway.

"Yes," she said.

An innocent look came into Jafar's eyes. "We will someday be khan and khanum of Dracon."

Raja looked into Jafar's eyes, but still held back her feelings. "I must go."

"We will see each other tomorrow then," said Jafar.

Raja nodded and then made her way to return to her room. Shamra was waiting for her. She saw the perplexed expression on Raja's face. "What happened?" she asked.

"He asked me to marry him."

"Really?"

"Yes."

"What did you say?"

"I said yes."

Shamra searched Raja's face. "Do you love him?"

"I don't know, but I think he's kind enough for me to learn to love him."

"You will," said Shamra.

The two sat in silence for a while, and then Raja spoke up. "What about Fedor?"

"He's coming, and he should be here shortly."

"Thank you for arranging that," said Raja. "Have you seen him?"

"Only from a distance, but he appeared well."

"Good."

At that moment, an escort led Fedor into the room. Raja was amazed. He looked like a different boy, neatly groomed and wearing fine clothes, not to mention his proper etiquette. She was thoroughly impressed.

"Hello, Fedor. How are you?"

He ran to her and bowed. "I missed you," he said.

"I missed you too. Are you happy with what you are doing?"

"Yes, and when I have a bit more training I get to be your errand boy."

"I would like that," said Raja.

"I have a gift for you," he said as he held out an arrangement of cut flowers.

"I can see that," said Raja as she took the flowers.

Fedor stood close to Raja and whispered, "Look inside, but don't let anyone see it."

Raja smelled the blossoms and looked between the stems. She whispered back, "How did you get this?"

"The captain gave it to me right before we left. She told me to wait a bit before I gave it to you."

Raja remembered that Fedor had been delayed inside the hut. Now she knew the reason. Then at that moment, an escort came to Fedor's side. Raja quickly held the flowers to her nose.

After only a short time to visit, Fedor was asked to leave with the escort. After Fedor left she ordered everyone out of the room except for Shamra. The servants and maids obeyed and left the room. As time went on Raja was being given more authority to do and say as she pleased. The khan saw her as very cooperative and happy, and so he placed upon her a higher level of trust. She was becoming more like a crown princess than a captured slave.

"What just happened?" asked Shamra.

"Do not tell anyone," whispered Raja, "but I think this might mean something."

"What means what?"

Raja took her doll from inside the flowers.

"Oh, it's beautiful. Is this the doll you told me about?"

"Yes, the pirate secretly gave it back to Fedor. I'm not sure why she would do that."

Raja counted the pearls on the doll as she always did. "Twenty-four pearls, none are missing."

"Did you say you got it from the tzarina?"

"The tzarina had given it to Pavel, who then gave it to me."

"Pavel gave it to you?"

"Yes."

The thought made Raja feel like crying and her eyes filled with tears. She wasn't expecting to ever see her doll again; the doll that always reminded her of Pavel. The circumstance was puzzling. Why would the captain give the doll up? Perhaps in the end, the captain did want to change, and this was the beginning. The doll certainly stirred up a lot of emotions inside of her. She buried her face in her pillow and cried.

Shamra comforted her. "It was good of the captain to do that. The captain probably knew how much the doll meant to you. You said yourself that the captain had told you that she liked you."

"Yes, she did say that, and yes, it was kind. I should be happy and thankful." Raja dried her tears. "Do you think it's wrong to carry it on me when I am to be married to Jafar?"

"No, I don't. It's only a doll, and he doesn't have to know. It represents a memory, and you don't have to give that up. And besides it also came from your tzarina mother."

Raja agreed with the logic. She hid the doll under her sash again. She wondered why the captain had said to hide it. Perhaps she didn't want people to know she had taken it in the first place. Perhaps she was changing.

It was time for dinner. Raja would sit beside Jafar, and later tonight she would dance with the prince. She would learn to love him if she didn't already.

Part 4

Prepare for Battle

Chapter 31

The Message

Arrangements were being made for Raja's wedding ceremony. Jafar had been giving her gifts of tea, baklava, and exotic jewelry of gold, silver, and precious stones. But above all, during an official ceremony inside the throne room, the khan had given her the crown jewel. She would wear the jewelry to the wedding ceremony. The ceremony would be elaborate and go on for three days with dancing, feasting, and rituals. It would happen in two more weeks. Until then, there would be dancing and feasting every evening. At the start of the two weeks of the celebration, Raja was to meet all the servants who would be serving or entertaining in order to give her approval of each.

Raja sat in her throne chair, which had a golden lion crest at the top. She was adorned in an elaborate costume with thick makeup on her face and she wore a large headpiece with strings of beads that covered her hair.

She met with her servants one by one. Each bowed as gracefully and honorably as they could, and then with eyes cast down, backed away and departed from her presence. An older man who was dressed in fine clothes now bowed before her. He slowly rose and backed away. Raja recognized the face.

"Stop!" she said. "Look at me."

Nervously, the man looked at Raja.

It was Kuzma!

"Go," said Raja. Kuzma bowed and retreated.

She was not expecting Kuzma to be here. She knew he didn't recognize her. She was overjoyed inside to know that he was still alive. Tonight she would consider what to do about it, as her present task occupied her full attention. She watched him leave the room.

The rest of the proceedings went without incident. Even Fedor was in the line of servants. He had been doing very well. He was still a slave, but in another sense he had gone from rags and starvation to riches and plenty.

That evening after dinner, Raja retreated to her room to think about Kuzma and the stories he had told in the village. She lay on her canopy bed and took out her doll. She counted the pearls again. It was something she did to soothe herself. She had been through a whirlwind of events, and her life right now seemed to be going at a very fast pace. What she truly thought in her heart was that she was too young to be married.

Seeing Kuzma had brought back emotions and memories from the past. The dream about the glowing sphere he had told her about while she was in the village was always in the back of her mind. She hoped for his sake that Kuzma could still, one day, reveal his dream to the person the monk had spoken about. It seemed like an important thing to do, although impossible in the present circumstances.

Raja ordered everyone out of her room and called for Shamra. She came in almost immediately and sat beside Raja on the bed.

"How are you doing?" asked Shamra, with softness in her voice.

"I'm not so sure again," said Raja.

"What's bothering you?"

"One of the servants is someone that I knew from the manor where I used to live."

"Who is it?"

"His name is Kuzma Basnya, and he was a storyteller."

"I've seen the khan's entertainer. That is probably the same person," said Shamra.

"And Kuzma plays the balalaika, which I'm sure would also delight the khan."

"Yes, I've seen him in the courtyard with the children," said Shamra. "He usually comes in the morning. But the khan is very protective of him. No one is allowed to approach his entertainer except the children. People have gotten thrown into prison for it."

"I'm sure the khan thinks Kuzma is more precious than golden jewels. His stories are so entertaining," said Raja. "He is probably worried that Kuzma will betray him by trying to escape. After all, it is not like he wanted to be here."

Both girls were grateful the khan was not treating Raja in the same way, although they were sure he still had his escorts keeping a constant eye on her.

"May I see your doll again?" asked Shamra.

"Of course."

"It's so lovely," said Shamra as she turned the doll over in her hands. She studied every detail of the doll, looking at all the stitching and embroidery. "This feels odd here," said Shamra, as she showed Raja the doll.

"Let me see." Raja took the doll and felt along the stitching. It did feel different. It wasn't smooth like the other side.

"I think there's something inside the doll," said Raja. "Get me a very small pair of scissors."

Shamra retrieved a pair of scissors, and Raja carefully cut open the stitches. Inside the doll was a small rolled paper.

"Oh, a message!" said Raja. She carefully took out the note so as not to ruin the doll and unrolled the paper. She read the message out loud.

Me sure ye be established as crown princess by now. If ye want to return to Zurkia send me the Dracian crown jewel inside the doll. Fer me to get help, I need the doll as proof that me is telling the truth. Write a note to show that ye trust me. Chamomile

"The pirate captain wrote this!" said Raja.

"Her name is Chamomile?"

"I remember her telling me that. But she actually calls herself Cham."

"How would she possibly return you to Zurkia?" asked Shamra.

"I don't know."

"How could you trust her? After all, she is just a pirate."

"That I know but . . ."

"And she doesn't explain anything about her plan. Don't you think if it were true and not a hoax she would have given you the doll herself?"

"No, not necessarily. She is too intelligent to have done that. I think she kept it from me on purpose."

"Why?"

"I have been acting like this is my new life, thinking that I would never be rescued. It helped to develop favor with the khan and now look at me."

"I think I'm understanding what you are saying."

"I have access to any jewel I want and can do things in my chamber without the escorts and servants watching."

"A definite advantage for Cham because she wants the jewel."

"True, but we'll be rescued."

Shamra took the note and examined it for herself in deep contemplation. She was worried about giving up the crown jewel. That could mean a lot of danger for Raja if she was found out.

"I can see what you are saying, but do you really want to send the crown jewel? She could just want the doll and the jewel for herself."

"Something tells me differently. You have to admit she did protect us and treat us fairly well."

Looking earnestly into Raja's face, Shamra wanted to say that Raja was right, but she felt frightened that they would be found out. Raja did not let Shamra's worried expression deter her from believing that Cham could be trusted.

"I don't think Cham wants to keep the doll," said Raja.

Shamra waited for another one of her logical explanations, as was always the case with Raja. "She wants to use the doll in some way."

"It really sounds like you want to take the chance and go through with the pirate's offer," said Shamra.

Turning the doll over in her hands, deep in thought for a few moments, Raja then spoke in a confident tone. "I've decided to trust her."

"It sounds like you've convinced yourself."

Raja nodded. She was willing to go by her instincts and take a chance.

Shamra looked questioningly into Raja's eyes. "So, I am understanding that if it were possible, you would like to return to Zurkia."

"Of course. I have only consented to marry Jafar because I have no choice."

Shamra understood how Raja felt. She herself deep down knew it wasn't right for Raja to stay in Dracon.

"But how are we going to get the crown jewel to the pirate captain who lives on the island?" asked Raja.

"If only we knew someone," said Shamra.

Raja moved over on the bed to make room for Shamra. The two girls turned on their sides to face each other. A few moments passed while they looked at each other. Finally Raja smiled as if the problem was solved. She spoke in a convincing light tone. "I've got the most brilliant idea . . . Kuzma can help us."

"Do you think that would work? He doesn't even know you are here," said Shamra.

"That's true, and from this point on, we can't let anyone know that we know each other. There has to be absolute secrecy."

"You have my word."

Raja thought about the predicament while she counted the embedded pearls on her doll out loud so Shamra could hear her. It reminded her of how Kuzma had taught her to count, but that now seemed like a long time ago. Raja finally turned to Shamra and said, "I think I have an idea. Could you please go and get Fedor?"

Shamra agreed at once and found Fedor. The two of them came back into Raja's room.

"Fedor," said Raja, "I have an errand for you to do."

"What is it?" asked Fedor as he bowed.

"Do you know who the storyteller is?"

"No," said Fedor.

"He is an older man whom we think goes regularly to the khan. He has a bit of a stoop and wears fine clothes. He also has a scar on his face."

"He sounds scary," said Fedor.

"He is actually a very nice man. He is my friend from our country. But you must not tell anyone that we know each other."

"Yes, my princess," said Fedor.

"My freedom from this place depends on that and that's why you have to be very secretive. Do you understand that?"

"Yes," said Fedor, who spoke his next words in a very worried manner. "But what will happen to me if you leave?"

"Don't worry. I would not leave you behind."

Fedor's expression relaxed, as Raja continued speaking.

"You must be very careful and cunning because you are going to be my spy."

"I am?" asked Fedor, whose eyes were getting more round by the second.

"Yes, don't make any mistakes. Our lives count on that."

Fedor agreed with a look of determination.

"Come back here tomorrow morning with a plate of baklava and tea."

Fedor bowed and left the room.

Later that evening Raja unknotted her scarf, which had been hidden around her waist ever since she was asked to remove it from her head. She put it to her face and thought about her mother. She hadn't even had the opportunity to see her, but she so much wanted to.

"What is it?" asked Fedor as he bowed.

"Do you know who the storyteller is?"

"No," said Fedor.

"He is an older man whom we think goes regularly to the khan. He has a bit of a stoop and wears fine clothes. He also has a scar on his face."

"He sounds scary," said Fedor.

"He is actually a very nice man. He is my friend from our country. But you must not tell anyone that we know each other."

"Yes, my princess," said Fedor.

"My freedom from this place depends on that and that's why you have to be very secretive. Do you understand that?"

"Yes," said Fedor, who spoke the next words in a very worried manner. "But what will happen to me if you leave?"

"Don't worry. I would not leave you behind."

Fedor's expression relaxed and Kaja continued speaking.

"You must be very careful and cunning because you are going to be my spy."

"I am?" asked Fedor, whose eyes were getting more round by the second.

"Yes, don't make any mistakes. Our lives count on that."

Fedor agreed with a look of determination.

"Come back here tomorrow morning with a plate of baklava and tea."

Fedor bowed and left the room.

Later that evening Kaja unknotted her scarf, which had been hidden around her waist ever since she was asked to remove it from her head. She put it to her face and thought about her mother. She hadn't even had the opportunity to see her, but she so much wanted to.

Chapter 32

Baklava and Tea

The next day, Fedor brought the baklava and tea to Raja's room as promised. Raja took her scarf, which she now hid inside her sleeve, and draped it over the baklava and tea.

"Find Kuzma," said Raja. "He is most likely to be in the courtyard with the children. Go up to him and say that you have a gift from the princess for his good service, and she would like him to partake of it immediately. Set the tray down and lift up the scarf."

Raja demonstrated her instructions with her scarf. "Ask him to take the tea first."

Fedor assured Raja he would. He bowed and was about to leave the room.

"Fedor," called Raja.

"Yes."

"Don't leave the scarf there."

"I won't."

"And empty the tea before you come back."

"Okay," he said and left the room with the tray in his hands.

He unobtrusively dodged around the numerous servants, escorts, and nobility who were going about their daily routines. The expansive courtroom was just as crowded as the halls. People were lounging and talking, and some were playing board games.

Fedor moved in and out of the crowds. He spotted a group of laughing children. A man was sitting cross-legged, entertaining them. As Fedor got closer, he saw the scar on the storyteller's face. He knew he had found him.

Fedor addressed Kuzma. "Storyteller, upon the request of the crown princess, I have a message for you."

Kuzma raised his head and looked at Fedor. "Go on," he said.

"I have a gift of baklava and tea. It is sent from the princess to reward you for your good service at the palace. She would like you to partake of it immediately."

"As she wishes," said Kuzma.

Fedor set the tray down beside the storyteller. For a moment the storyteller was stunned. It was the scarf he saw. He recognized it. Could it be Raja's scarf? The memory of the attack on the jousting field came back to Kuzma. Was it possible she had been captured and now was the princess of Dracon?

Before Kuzma could remove the scarf, Fedor lifted it as Raja had shown him. "Please, the tea," said Fedor.

Kuzma looked at the boy and slowly raised the tea bowl. A small folded note lay under the tea bowl. Kuzma discreetly picked up the note and slipped it inside his sleeve. He proceeded to pour his tea and eat the baklava.

"Tell her thank you very much," said Kuzma. "I'll be waiting for more tomorrow, and could you please bring me chamomile tea. It's my favorite."

Fedor bowed and left the courtyard.

Kuzma finished telling his stories to the children and left to find a place that was private, so he could read the note. When he opened the note, he was surprised to find a string of pearls nestled inside its creases.

He silently read to himself.

Kuzma, it's Princess Raja, but I'm referred to as Princess Diamonique. Find a merchant who will deliver my crown jewel and doll to the pirate captain on Kulaly Island. I will explain later. You will have it tomorrow. Pay the merchant with this string of royal pearls and say he will be further rewarded after he delivers the jewel.

"Raja," said Kuzma to himself. "This is just like you."

Kuzma turned the pearls over in his hand. He could tell they were very valuable. Yes, he would do that. He didn't know the plan, but he trusted her.

It was always Kuzma's duty to go to the bazaar and bring back items for the khan. On his next trip, he would find a merchant, someone he knew from the past and whom he could trust. For now, he would wait for the crown jewel.

The next morning, the tray and scarf had come back to Raja and Shamra, and Raja lay on the bed looking at the oval red ruby that had been given to her by Jafar.

"This is the most valuable crown jewel," said Raja.

"Are you still sure you trust the pirate captain?" asked Shamra.

"I do. And even if I'm wrong, it is worth a try. What would I have to lose?"

"Jafar would be wondering where it had disappeared to."

"I can wear something else on the wedding day."

"And if he asks about it?"

"I will say it disappeared from my room."

"Then I might be suspected," said Shamra.

"True, then I will just say that I like my other jewel necklace better. After all, I can wear what I want if I'm the crown princess."

"I hope that works."

Raja hoped she wouldn't be in that situation in the first place. She now desperately wanted to be rescued. Raja took her doll from her sash and opened up the side. She carefully stuffed the red ruby inside the doll and then included the note of trust to Cham. After stitching the doll back together, she examined it to make sure the bump from the jewel wasn't too noticeable in case it somehow got into the wrong hands.

Satisfied with her work, Raja gave the doll to Shamra. "You can have the honors. Put the doll inside the teapot."

Shamra made sure the teapot was dry and then placed the doll inside.

"Perfect," said Raja as she laid the scarf over the tray which held the baklava and teapot. "Fedor should be here any minute."

Fedor arrived on time and Raja told him that a jewel was inside the doll and to be very careful about carrying out all of her instructions. He agreed and set out to find Kuzma. Upon entering the courtyard, he again saw Kuzma with the children and set out to cross the floor. Today, there seemed to be more people in the audience and he had to make sure not to bump into anyone.

Suddenly, an escort stood right in front of Fedor, blocking his path. "What do you have there?" he asked.

Without looking up, Fedor answered. "A gift of baklava and tea for the storyteller."

"I'm thirsty. Pour me some tea."

"The crown princess said it was for the storyteller."

Raising his voice, he said, "Pour me some!"

Fedor set the tray down on the floor, feeling his legs starting to tremble. He lifted the teapot and tilted the spout into the cup. Then he stood up still not looking at the escort. "I regret to say escort, there is no tea inside the pot."

"What kind of a servant serves with no tea in the pot!" The escort stooped down and took the lid off of the teapot. Reaching his hand into the pot, he pulled out the doll. Fedor bit his lower lip. His heart started to beat fast and he wanted to run to where he would never be found.

"What is this?" asked the escort.

Memories of his past on the streets of Kazan flooded Fedor's mind. The only way out of being accused of stealing was to run. He could run out of this palace and into Baku. He knew how to hide and he could return to his old way of life.

Fedor caught the eyes of Kuzma looking at him. There was something in that face that spoke to him. No, he was not going to run. He was going to be brave and answer the question intelligently. He was not going to disappoint Princess Raja, let alone have them all thrown into the dungeon.

"It is a gift for the storyteller from the princess."

"Why is it in the teapot?" asked the escort with a very straight face.

Fedor tried not to falter in his speech and answered as quickly as he could while trying to think of an answer. He stammered a little bit and hoped it wouldn't be the last sentence he spoke.

"She, she . . . likes to joke. She wanted it to be a humorous surprise for the storyteller."

Turning the doll over, the escort looked at it. Fedor watched his every move as his fingers traced over the doll. Looking up at the escort, their eyes met. At that moment, Fedor held a straight face, determined not to show any fear.

"A peculiar way to present a gift," said the escort.

"Prince Jafar likes to hear the princess tell him about the humorous things she does. It delights him."

The answer seemed to satisfy the escort. He smiled and then spoke, as if addressing himself. "An odd sense of humor indeed. The prince will have quite a task at hand." The escort dropped the doll back in the teapot. "After you deliver the gift, bring me some tea."

Fedor bowed. "Yes, of course, escort." Feeling extremely relieved, Fedor then walked over to Kuzma and held the teapot in front of him. Kuzma took the doll from inside the pot and then forced a jolly laugh. Kuzma put the doll in his pouch and stuffed the pastry into his mouth.

"Thank the princess for the baklava."

Fedor bowed and then left the room with the tray.

The baklava was good, thought Kuzma, and it helped him to partially forgive Raja for the risk she'd just taken. No doubt the jewel was hidden inside the doll. However, even though he felt a bit upset over the risk, the jewel had gotten safely to Kuzma and for that he could be thankful.

Kuzma sent the children away early and went to his chamber. He took the doll from his sash and pressed down on it in the center. Yes, he was right, the jewel was inside. He decided to write a note for the merchant. He didn't know whom he would find, but Kuzma hoped he would be at the right place at the right time. He took his feather quill, dipped it in the ink, and wrote a message.

Do this as a favor for your old friend. Deliver this doll to the pirate captain on Kulaly Island. These pearls are your reward. After you deliver the doll, you will be further rewarded. Kuzma

Kuzma folded the note and wrapped it around the doll with the string of pearls.

Chapter 33

The Treat After the Story

Merchants greeted Kuzma as he walked by the various stands in the city of Baku. He was still well known from his former years when he had traded as a merchant. He became more fluent in the various languages that he knew, as he always spent time mingling with the sellers and buyers. He endeavored to look interested in buying the goods, but at the same time kept an eye on what his main purpose was, namely, to find a merchant. His escort seemed fairly relaxed, and of course, had no suspicion of what he was doing.

As it turned out, he saw more than one merchant whom he knew. He would have to carefully consider who would be the best person to carry out the request. He wasn't sure of any of them, but then he noticed someone else he knew. He was a merchant fisherman, humble, whom Kuzma thought was always trustworthy. He was on the poor side, which would make him an even better choice. Of course, the merchant would have to be brave in order to deal with pirates, but this merchant was brave. In fact, he remembered that the fisherman had once traded with the pirates on that island. That seemed at little far-fetched, but the fisherman claimed it was true.

Kuzma approached the fisherman merchant. They greeted each other exuberantly, and Kuzma started in on a conversation to hold the man's interest. They chatted for some time, and when Kuzma saw that his escort was occupied with something else, he leaned into the fisherman. "I have a deal for you, but tell no one," said Kuzma, in a low voice. "It will make you a rich man. Take what I'm going to give you."

The escort looked their way. Kuzma continued his lively conversation. When it seemed like the escort was not paying attention, Kuzma gave the fisherman his pouch while continuing the lively conversation. The fisherman slipped it over his shoulder. Kuzma adjusted a second pouch that he had been carrying over his other shoulder. The two talked for another minute and then parted. Kuzma finished his browsing, purchased some incense, and returned to the Dragomir Palace.

Days later, Fedor was again with Raja in her room. They arranged the baklava and tea on the tray in just the right way. Then Raja draped her scarf over the arrangement.

"You are like my spy," said Raja, smiling at Fedor.

"Do you think I'd make a good spy?"

"Yes, indeed, you would."

"Do spies sometimes get caught?'

"Yes, so that is why you must always be vigilant and alert. It would be a terrible thing if you were caught."

Raja didn't want Fedor to become overly confident or too relaxed with his mission. He had continued to pass Raja's notes on to Kuzma now for more than a week. The notes had been encouraging to Raja, and had helped her believe that what she had done with the jewel was the wisest choice. And during the week, Raja had sent more jewels to Kuzma so he could reward the merchant.

Fedor stood at the entrance ready to leave with the tray of tea and baklava.

"See you in a while," said Raja.

"Yes, my princess."

Fedor left the room and ventured to take the hidden note to Kuzma once again.

Kuzma was glad to see Fedor. "Ah, my favorite servant," he said, as he ritually lifted the scarf, found the note under the baklava, and then slipped it into his sleeve.

"Stay this time and listen to my story." The storyteller motioned for Fedor to sit in front of the group.

Fedor considered the offer and agreed. He had never been told a story before. Kuzma began.

Marissea the Doll

There once was a girl named Jamelia, who was born of a fisherman and his wise wife. When the girl became eight, her mother gave her a beautiful little doll. The mother said that it had been her doll when she was a girl, and that the doll was very special to her. The mother said that the doll's name was Marissea. She asked her daughter to take care of the doll and to be kind to it as a way of honoring her mother. The daughter agreed that she would always be kind to the doll.

One day, the mother became ill and the father had no fire to light the wood in the stove. So, the fisherman asked the girl to go to a neighboring village and bring back some embers. The girl agreed to do this and took Marissea the Doll with her. While she was walking in the woods, she became lost, and she thought the wolves would eat her. The doll remembered Jamelia's kindness and it became human. Marissea told Jamelia that because she had chosen to honor her mother, she would help her. So Marissea showed Jamelia the way back to the path. When they were on the path again, the girl thanked Marissea the Doll, and it went back to what it was before. Jamelia sang a song to the doll and straightened out its dress.

Jamelia walked on and met a wolf that she had been dreading all along. Again, the doll remembered Jamelia's kindness and became human. Marissea told the girl to not be afraid, but to stand beside her in front of the wolf. Jamelia did so, and light poured from Marissea's eyes, blinding the wolf. The wolf ran away, and the girl thanked Marissea before it went back to being a doll. Jamelia rocked the doll in her arms and sang it a song.

The girl was almost out of the woods and felt she would be safe when a witch appeared out of nowhere. The witch said that she would eat her, but upon looking at Jamelia, she was so beautiful, the witch decided she would give her one chance to free herself. The witch told Jamelia that if she answered her question with wisdom she would let her go. But, not really believing that the girl would answer wisely, the witch asked her what she would want most of all in life.

Jamelia thought the question was very difficult, as there were many answers, and so she was about to give up in despair. The doll became invisible and whispered something in the girl's ear. Jamelia smiled and said that the one thing she would want was for the witch to let her go. Angry with the girl, the witch said that she had answered wisely and let her go. After Marissea changed back into a doll, Jamelia gently wrapped a blanket around the doll to keep it warm, and sang it another song.

Continuing to the village, the girl got some embers in a pot. Several villagers walked her safely home. When she got home, she gave her father the embers and the mother recovered from the warmth of the fire. Then Jamelia sang a song to her doll and carefully tucked it into bed. Because of Jamelia's acts of kindness to her doll, she grew up to be the kindest and most prosperous person in the country.

The children clapped after Kuzma had finished his story. He handed out treats to the children. Fedor took his treat and thanked the storyteller. Fedor bowed and then left.

He looked at his treat while he was walking back to Raja's room. It didn't look like anything he had eaten before. He tasted it. It was delicious. He took another bite and studied his treat while he ate it.

Suddenly, a hand snatched the scarf, and the person who took the scarf ran into the crowd. All that Fedor saw was a black cape. Fedor ran through the crowd, but there was no evidence of the person or the scarf anywhere.

Chapter 34

Stones in the Wall

"I'm sorry, your highness, that your scarf was taken. I was eating my treat and not paying attention." Standing in Raja's chamber, Fedor's eyes were on his feet in shame.

"Don't blame yourself. It probably would have happened anyway. Do you know whether it was a man or a woman?"

"No, the person went too fast."

"But the person was wearing a black cape?"

"Yes."

Raja doubted that she would see her scarf again. If the person were caught, he or she would definitely be accused of thievery. She felt extremely disappointed; first it was her jewel, now her scarf, and she didn't know if she would ever get her doll back.

"May I still be your errand boy?"

"Of course," said Raja and gave Fedor a little hug. "But you need to leave now, because I have to get ready for tonight."

"Okay, I'll watch for the scarf."

"Thanks."

After Fedor left the room, Raja starting thinking about the evening. Tonight was the first day of her wedding ceremony. She was to attend the feast with Jafar, and the two of them would mingle with the guests. They had plans to give each of the guests a silver ring signifying complete happiness with their approaching union.

Shamra helped her dress in her ceremonial garment. She wore her headpiece with the green, orange, and purple emeralds. Her dress had puffy sleeves, a gold, fitted bodice, and a billowy skirt. She put a robe over top of her dress and would take it off when the ceremonies began. The outfit was beautiful, but the more simple clothing that she used to wear was much more to her taste.

Shamra led Raja to the feast and guided her to the side of Jafar. They greeted each other respectfully and commenced their duties. Raja was glad of Jafar's ability to hold interesting conversations and the fact that he knew a variety of languages. She herself understood parts of the different languages being spoken and was becoming more fluent with the daily instruction she received.

The hall was filled mostly with nobility, but the guests also included merchants and craftsmen. She could see that the khan was thoroughly enjoying the event, and thankfully he didn't seem to be watching her all that much.

In the midst of the crowd, a girl caught her attention. She was wearing a black cape, and her face was partially covered with a scarf. Raja thought the scarf looked like her scarf. Raja slowly moved away from Jafar and worked her way toward the girl. When Raja had nearly approached her, the girl moved away. Raja followed her, and the girl continued to move away. They dodged their way through the crowd, and the girl disappeared around the corner. Raja stepped up her pace to follow the girl.

She had to know who had taken her scarf and why. They went through a maze of corridors. She had never been in this part of the palace before and wasn't sure if she could find her way back. Suddenly, the girl stopped and turned around to face Raja. She whipped the scarf from her face. Raja was flabbergasted. It was Hannah.

"I should have known. You always find me," said Raja, feeling a little out of breath.

"We have no time to lose. Follow me."

"Why are you here?"

"To rescue you! Come on!"

"But ... I have to ...."

"Tell me later. We cannot linger in the hall."

Raja agreed and followed Hannah.

Hannah led her farther down the corridor and then into an alcove. She knelt and removed some stones from the wall. The opening was large enough for them to crawl through. Raja took a torch from the wall and went first. Hannah followed and then replaced the stones in the wall before going on. As they crawled farther through the tunnel, the space got large enough for them to stand up.

"Let's talk," said Hannah as she turned to face Raja.

The two sat across from each other.

"You really surprised me," said Raja. "I'm so glad to see you."

"I hope you weren't losing faith."

"Perhaps a little," said Raja.

"Never lose faith," said Hannah. "As you can see, I am here to take you out of this place."

"How did you know about this secret passage?" asked Raja.

"My father has connections with the khan. They deal in illegal ways, and so the khan gave my father a map of all the secret passages in the Dragomir Palace. I knew that he had the map and I drew my own copy of it."

Raja listened with raised eyebrows and wide eyes as Hannah continued.

"Listen, we have to go fast or people will suspect your absence."

"I can't go with you now. I can't leave the others behind," said Raja. "I just can't do that."

"I suspected this might be the case. Who is coming with you?"

"A girl named Shamra and a boy named Fedor. Kuzma is here too."

"Kuzma?"

"Yes."

"I thought he might be here," said Hannah. "Come with me through the tunnels so you know the passages."

Raja and Hannah continued through the passageways, which turned out to be a maze of small tunnels. Hannah showed her the numerous secret entryways that either led into a room, stairs, or another tunnel. Hannah pointed out the places on the map with each new area they went to.

"Let's go back," said Hannah.

"How am I going to remember this?" asked Raja.

"You can have the map," said Hannah. "I have it memorized."

"Thanks."

The two retraced the route they had taken and then crawled along the last part of the passageway. Raja's knees were getting sore, and she was glad they were at the end.

"What is your plan?" asked Raja.

"Tomorrow, I will be in the halls acting as a servant. Come at noon and take a piece of baklava. A note will be placed under the pastry."

Raja agreed to the plan. "Where are you staying?" she asked.

"I can't tell you."

"Why not?"

"Because what you don't know you can't reveal in case there is any suspicion."

"I understand," said Raja.

Hannah's face grew serious. "But I can tell you this—prepare for battle."

Raja felt worried. She wondered whether Hannah meant here or in Kazan. "What do you mean by that?"

"That's all I can tell you. You need to go now."

"Okay."

"Raja."

"Yes."

"Here's your scarf."

"Thanks," she said and tucked it away.

"And Raja, there's one more thing. Here's your doll."

Feeling completely surprised, Raja took the doll.

"How did you get my doll?"

"That's a long story, but there's a note in it."

Raja hid the doll under her sash along with the map.

"I'll see you tomorrow," said Hannah.

"I'll see you tomorrow," said Raja.

Raja took the stones out from the wall and crawled out.

Thankfully, nobody was in the hallway. She put the stones back and made her way to her room. She made a few wrong turns, but managed in a short time to find her way out of the maze of corridors. She arrived at her room and quickly took the note out of the doll. Tears formed in her eyes as she read it. She dried her tears and went back to the feast.

She found Jafar, who seemed not to have missed her. The two continued their ceremonial feasting throughout the evening. Raja acted as if she was a very happy bride-to-be.

Chapter 35

Broken-Hearted

The map that Hannah had given Raja had a lot of detail and was hard to read. However, for the most part, Raja could understand it. Raja had told Shamra about how she had gone through the secret passageways with Hannah. The two girls privately studied the map the next morning while lying on top of Raja's bed and taking turns holding Raja's doll.

"This is where the secret passage starts and these lines show where it leads to," said Raja.

"That's amazing. Who would have thought all of this existed in the palace?"

"It is amazing. See, the map tells you where to look and what to look for at each new secret entry. The tunnel that I was in leads to a set of spiral stairs that goes to another room. This room has a rotating stone wall and goes into another tunnel, which leads into another room. Here, there are vertical stairs hidden underneath the stone floor. These stones can be removed and are in the north corner. The vertical stairs lead to another tunnel, which divides into three more tunnels, but only one of them leads to the outside. And that's this one."

"Why is it so complicated?"

"In case someone discovers the passageway, they will have a difficult time entering the palace. And it would also make it difficult for someone to leave the palace if they weren't supposed to."

Raja traced the route with her fingers, starting from her chamber. She could see that there were other passages drawn on the map as well, but she didn't think she needed to worry about them. She would memorize every detail of this part of the map before the escape.

"There was something in the doll," said Raja, a bit hesitantly.

"What was it?"

"A note from Pavel."

"What did it say?"

Raja took the note from the doll. "But you must swear not to tell anyone."

"I swear."

Raja showed Shamra the note, which displayed a mix of letters. In between giggles she read the note to Shamra.

Ll'I eb ta eht dne fo eht lennut.

"That sounds funny," said Shamra. "What does it mean?"

"It's our secret code."

Shamra smiled. "You made a secret code with Pavel?"

"I know that might sound a bit strange, but it was fun to do."

"I'm curious about it. Are you going to tell me how to decode it?"

"No, we swore secrecy to each other."

A slightly disappointed look came over Shamra's face. "I understand."

Seeing the disappointment, Raja said, "We can make up our own."

Shamra's smile returned.

Raja folded the map and note and tucked them inside the doll. "We should go to the hall to find Hannah."

Shamra looked at the hourglass. "You're right. It's noon just now."

Shamra and Hannah made their way to the hall. Raja looked among the servants. No one resembled Hannah. "I don't see her," whispered Raja, looking at each and every servant.

A boy-servant approached them. "Please take one," said the servant as he presented them with baklava.

Raja recognized the undisguised voice immediately. She could then see the face had been darkened with makeup.

"Thank you, I must say your attire suits you today," said Raja.

"I take it that is your attempt to be humorous."

"Maybe."

"Very funny. Take the middle piece."

Raja took the pastry and slipped the note in her sash. The disguised servant bowed and left. Shamra and Raja went back to the chamber. Raja immediately opened the note and read it to Shamra.

Be in the kitchen tomorrow just before sunset. Dismiss all of the servants.

Raja looked at Shamra. “This only gives me one day to let Kuzma know about the escape.”

“What are you going to do?” asked Shamra.

“Write back immediately.”

Raja began writing Kuzma a note while saying it out loud.

Kuzma, wait at the hall entrance for me just before sunset. We will escape together. Remember your promise to the monk.

“I hope this works,” said Shamra.

“Me too.”

Raja called for Fedor right away and explained to him what he needed to do. The next morning, Fedor delivered the note, and somehow Kuzma had gotten a note back to Fedor. When Fedor found Raja she was by herself. She took the note and read it to herself.

It is not meant to be. The khan is not well and wants me constantly by his side. If I were to leave, it would jeopardize your safe escape. Kuzma.

Raja was broken-hearted. She loved Kuzma. Tears flooded her eyes.

“Fedor, please find Shamra for me.”

Fedor bowed and hurried to find Shamra.

Minutes later, Shamra came to the chamber, and Raja buried her head in her lap. In between sobs, Raja told Shamra about the note and all the reasons why she wanted Kuzma to come back to Zurkia. She loved his jolly nature and interesting stories. He had taught her so much. And didn't he care about the dream? Surely, it was meant to be.

Raja continued crying, catching her breath in between sobs. Shamra comforted her in the best way that she could and told her things might work out differently in the future. It needn't always have to stay this way.

Chapter 36

Fooled

Raja was alone in her chamber, and was dressed for the third and final day of her wedding ceremony. Her headpiece adorned a beautiful lace veil that would later cover her face. Tonight, there would be solemn rituals to signify a long life, success, and wealth. Then the couple would each go into a private prayer room for one hour to further meditate on what would bring them a healthy and prosperous marriage.

The wind from the sea blew on Raja's face as she looked out the palace window from her chamber. The palace was built on the edge of a steep hill next to the shores of the Khvalyn Sea. The sea was magnificent, topped with white crests gamboling alongside the dark indigo hue.

She couldn't stop thinking that either tonight would be her last night here, or tonight she would be wed to Jafar. She knew it didn't help to worry about it and thought of the story that Fedor had passed on to her after hearing it from Kuzma. She began to trust that she would be shown the right path. She took out her doll from her sash and counted the pearls to comfort herself. Her eyes grew watery again thinking about Kuzma.

The sun was just about to set. It was time to go. Shamra came in and lowered the veil on Raja's headpiece. Raja left everything behind except her doll and scarf, which were hidden in her pouch under her dress. Fedor and the twin maids entered her room and accompanied Raja down the corridors. The trail of her dress flowed behind her on the floor.

But before entering the ceremony room, Raja said she wanted to check the food preparations for after the wedding. She was then escorted to the kitchen. She went in and ordered everyone out except for Fedor and Shamra and said that she wanted to have privacy while she checked the food.

"Are you sure this is the right place?" asked Shamra.

"Yes, Hannah's note said to meet here."

"But the escape passage is in the alcove."

"I know."

Just then, the three of them heard a knock. It was coming from the pantry. Raja rushed into the pantry. The knock was coming from beneath the floor. She pried on a stone tile with the back of a large spoon. The stone loosened, and she lifted it up. Underneath was a wooden trap door. Pulling more stones away, she finally lifted the door.

Hannah crawled out. "Did I surprise you?"

"Only a little," said Raja, who made introductions between Shamra, Fedor, and Hannah. The three quickly exchanged formalities.

Then Hannah got very serious. "We need to hurry. Let's exchange clothes."

"Fedor, turn around," said Raja.

"Are you twins?" asked Fedor, his jaw dropping.

"No, hush, turn around," said Raja.

Hannah and Raja put on one another's clothes. Then Raja and Shamra adjusted the wedding headpiece on Hannah's head and lowered the veil. Raja put the piece of jewelry that she was wearing around Hannah's neck.

"Where does this passage lead to?" asked Raja, feeling confused.

"It leads straight to the other passage that we were on before. You can't get lost." Hannah looked at Raja with a serious expression. "Can you do it?"

Raja nodded in return with a slight smile. "I can do it."

"You must hurry."

Raja lowered herself into the passage.

"It's so dark," said Fedor.

"You'll be fine," said Hannah, as she handed Raja a burning lantern.

Shamra and Fedor got into the passageway. The trap door was closed, and the stone tiles were replaced.

Hannah swiftly left the room and told the servants they could resume their duties. Through the commotion of the many servants, no one noticed that Fedor and Shamra were missing.

The twin maids escorted Hannah to the wedding ceremony. She stood in front of the entrance way as if she were Raja. No one would be able to tell the difference. Their voices were even the same and they carried themselves in the same manner.

Hannah kneeled before the sacerdos suffering through all the rituals, giving all of the appropriate identity answers, of which she had been well prepared for. She made sure to only look at Jafar a few moments at a time giving him a quick little smile. Jafar caught the looks and returned a smile each time.

She was certain the ceremony so far had lasted over an hour. Besides her knees getting sore, the most difficult thing was saying yes in acceptance to marrying Jafar. But being an imposter, she didn't think the marriage would be legal, at least she hoped not.

The two were then led to the prayer room to allow the couple their hour of devotion before the lifting of the wedding veil in front of the guests.

Before going into the prayer room, Jafar looked into Hannah's eyes, which were partially concealed under the veil. "My new bride, how are you doing?"

Hannah whispered, "Fine, I love you." She smiled, feeling amused by her reply.

Jafar wondered why Raja hadn't said that before, but returned the words. "I love you, too." He picked up the jeweled necklace that was around Hannah's neck. He was confused as to why she hadn't worn the other crown jewel, which was much larger and more valuable. "Why did you wear this jewel?"

Hannah didn't know anything about the necklaces. She tried to think of a quick answer. She looked at the necklace.

"The purple sapphire is my favorite jewel," said Hannah. "I love the color purple."

Jafar thought about that answer and then said, "It's my favorite, too."

Hannah smiled and then turned to go into her private prayer room. No one else would be allowed in the room, as it was only used for prayer by a wedding couple. Hannah locked the door behind her and quickly took down a large picture from the wall. Then, removing some stones to make a hole large enough for her to crawl through, she went into a secret passageway. She replaced the stones and made her way through the passageway to the stables. She had to go down several stairs and through at least two other secret entries.

At the stables, Boris had Raja's white horse and Jafar's black horse ready to ride. Boris had acted as one of the stable grooms and had told the other grooms they could attend the wedding ceremony.

Hannah took off her headpiece and threw it to the side. She had fooled them all. Mounting her horse, she put on her hood, and the two of them were off. Riding as swiftly as she could, Hannah took the lead with her white horse. Once out of the city, they still had enough light to gallop like the wind toward the ship.

Chapter 37

Mistakes on the Map

Crawling through the passageway underneath the Dragomir Palace, Raja led the way. Fedor thought the journey was adventurous, but Shamra thought it was agonizing. However, Shamra was holding her tongue simply because she appreciated being rescued and didn't want to complain. Both of the girls would have liked it more if their knees weren't sore from crawling on the rock surface. Despite the obstacle, Raja thought they were making good time. Then to Raja's dismay her knee jabbed into the sharp edge of a rock. It hurt. She felt her knee and could tell she had cut it.

"I cut my knee," said Raja, knowing she had to bandage the cut if they were to still make good time. "I really don't want to use my scarf."

"I have a linen cloth under my sash," said Fedor. He quickly pulled it out and handed it to Shamra, who handed it to Raja.

"Thank you, Fedor. What would I do without you?"

"Good thinking, Fedor," said Shamra.

Raja bandaged her knee and the three of them went on, but not quite as fast as before. They reached the spiral stairs that led into the room with the rotating wall. They had no problem turning the wall and continued walking through the next tunnel. They finally came to the next room and searched for the hidden stones on the floor.

"None of these stones seem to be loose," said Raja feeling exasperated, as she tried prying each stone with her hands. She knew they must not spend a lot of time trapped inside the tunnel. The three of them went over each stone again and again, trying to find the right location.

"This stone is loose!" said Fedor.

"Show me!" said Raja as she rushed over to his side.

Raja and Fedor worked to loosen the stone and sure enough it came out. It wasn't exactly in the north end as described on the map. Nevertheless, the three managed to clear the entryway and they made their way down the vertical ladder and into another tunnel. The tunnel eventually divided into three tunnels, as shown on the map.

"I'm quite sure it's this one," said Raja and led them into the east tunnel. The tunnel got smaller and smaller and they had to again crawl on their hands and knees. They finally came to the end.

"This is obviously the wrong tunnel. We need to go back," said Raja.

Fedor had to lead the way back. When they reached the intersection, they instead took the west tunnel. As they walked along with Raja leading the way, they eventually had to crawl again, but this time the tunnel didn't come to a dead end. Raja was determined to check the map when she got out of the tunnel.

Raja, Shamra, and Fedor finally reached the end of the passageway that came out on the side of the hill below the Dragomir Palace. A large rock and dense shrubs camouflaged the entrance.

"We've made it," said Raja.

"We actually made it?" asked Fedor.

"Yes, we did."

Coming out of the hole, a hand came to Raja's side.

"Pavel!" said Raja. Tears ran down her cheeks as she cried with joy. After setting down her lantern, she rushed to hug Pavel. "I thought I had lost you forever."

"Are you all right?" asked Pavel.

"Yes."

"I'm so glad to see you unharmed," said Pavel.

"I am grateful," said Raja, as she looked into his face, which held sincere concern.

"We have no time to waste. We must leave at once. Follow me," said Pavel.

"Wait, may I do something first?"

"What is it?"

"I want to check something on my map."

"Okay, but hurry," said Pavel, as he looked up at the palace with a worried expression.

Raja quickly got out the map of the passageways and checked it. Indeed, it looked like she had been right and the map wrong. She concluded that people do make mistakes. Or perhaps, it was done on purpose as a defense tactic. She'd have to discuss it with Hannah.

"Are you ready?" asked Pavel.

"Yes, but first I must introduce you to my friends, Shamra and Fedor," said Raja.

Pavel and Fedor bowed during the formalities, while Shamra curtsied.

Pavel tried to be as polite as he could but was definitely getting anxious. "Let's go," he said.

"Where are we going?"

"To the pirate's ship."

"Cham's pirate ship?"

"Yes, but she calls herself Chamomile."

"She told you her full name?"

"I'll explain later, as we really need to get going."

"Okay," said Raja who felt pleased knowing Cham must have trusted Pavel enough to tell him about her past, since sharing her full name was a very personal thing for her to do. Raja hoped it was a step toward change for her.

The four started climbing down the hill towards the seashore. Part of the descent was steep but they all managed without too much trouble. They ran slowly down the shoreline of the sea.

Raja called out. "I'm assuming Cham found you."

"Yes, at the manor."

"So you trusted her?"

"After I read your very poetic note and saw the doll, yes."

"What did you write that was so poetic?" asked Shamra.

"I have the note right here," said Pavel as he stopped running and took the note from his sash. "May I show it to Shamra?"

Agreeing, Raja took the note from Pavel and showed it to Shamra.

Smiling, Shamra read it out loud.

In grace, tell Lord Pavel to not delay,
and join your two different strengths together.
Chamomile, I know you will find a way,
as did Angelica with her feather.

"True, only you could have written this beautiful poem," said Shamra.

Pavel put the note back in his sash and the three of them picked up their pace again. Raja was so glad that Cham's crafty plan, mixed with her own convincing poem, had all worked out.

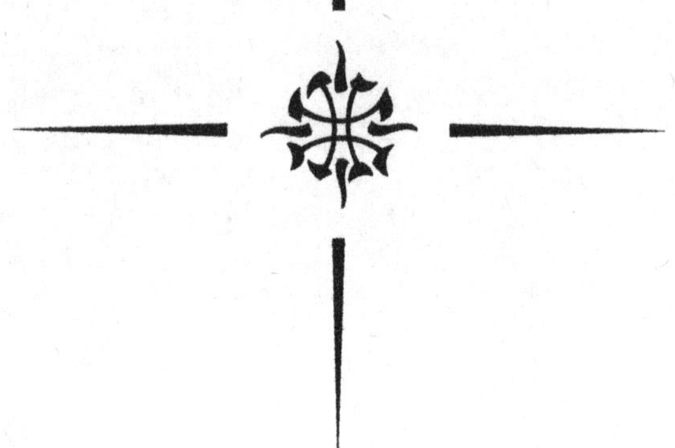

Chapter 38

Meeting of Orsus

The two parties arrived at the port of Baku at the same time. Hannah and Boris dismounted and tied the horses to a hitching post. The two groups ran up the wharf and scrambled up the plank onto the pirate ship. The pirates immediately lifted their anchor and set sail. They raised the Zurkian flag, which was the color red with a white circle in the center. Pavel had taken the flag from a Zurkian ship and attached it to the mast on Cham's ship. They were on their way back to Zurkia.

"Everyone, this is Shamra and this is Fedor," said Raja as a group of people assembled on the deck.

The group, including Cham, greeted the two newcomers.

"Why didn't Kuzma come?" asked Pavel.

Raja noticed that Cham was going to say something, but then didn't.

"He didn't want to jeopardize our safety," said Raja with a sad look.

"That would be like Kuzma, always doing something for someone else," said Pavel.

Raja turned to Cham. "Thanks for your part in rescuing us."

Cham nodded and then replied. "Yer welcome."

Pavel spoke to the whole group. "We need to talk." He then looked at Cham for direction.

"Come into me aftercastle. It'll be a bit crowded but we'll have privacy."

Everyone crowded into the aftercastle. Pavel then addressed Raja. "I have terrible news."

"What is it?"

"I think you will be needing this," said Pavel. He held up Raja's double-edged sword. "We found this in the alley after you were missing."

Raja took her sword. "And why will I be needing it?"

"The throne has been taken over by the Dark Prince. And your mother is in the dungeon of Kazan Castle."

Raja was aghast. "How did it happen?"

"The prince denied the accusations that were made against him when you were captured the first time, and there was pressure on the tzarina to release him from prison. The Dark Prince made amends with your mother over a period of time with sincere apologies. He brought her gifts of all sorts. One of the gifts was a large, oval, red ruby. He received your mother's forgiveness and then presented Hannah to your mother. The Dark Prince told the tzarina that he had rescued Raja from the Tyhets. His plan was working."

"What did my mother do with Hannah?" asked Raja as she looked at her cousin, finding it hard to believe that her mother could be fooled. But, on the other hand, Raja knew their resemblance was striking.

"Your mother had never seen Hannah before, and she thought Hannah was her daughter. She made Hannah the Princess of Kazan, and after that it was easy for the Dark Prince to capture the tzarina and take over the throne."

Raja addressed Hannah. "Are you sitting on the throne in Zurkia now?"

"Yes, along with my father," she said. "But, understand it is really my father who wants to rule."

"But, it is not just Hannah's father," said Pavel. "The Kazan Castle is being influenced by another relative."

"And they seem to be the catalyst behind the capture of the throne," said Hannah.

"I see," said Raja. "The situation is very serious. I really hope my mother will live."

"I'm sorry, Raja, that it had to be that way," said Hannah. "My father still does not suspect me. He thinks I am elsewhere right now."

"I understand," said Raja. "It is important to keep your father believing that you are on his side."

Hannah smiled sympathetically. "But I did convince him to spare your mother's life."

"Thank you."

Cham interrupted the conversation.

"Did you say that one of the gifts to the tzarina was an oval red ruby?"

"That's correct," said Pavel.

"That would have been the crown ruby from Dracon that I sold to the Grand Padesha Tzoycha at Port Alexandra."

"Who then sold it to the Dark Prince?" asked Pavel.

"It seems to be the case," said Cham.

"Where did you get it?" asked Pavel.

"From Raja," said Cham.

Pavel looked at Raja.

"It was payment to rescue me," said Raja.

"Well, things can certainly go around," said Pavel. He waited a few seconds and then started in on the conversation again. "We are going to rescue the tzarina as soon as we can. But first, we need to take back the throne."

"What's yer plan?" asked Cham.

"Ever since Raja was captured, and even before that, my father has been building up his army. He has trained peasants who are eager to fight with him. The peasants do not like the prince because he has increased the taxes, which have made life harder for them," said Pavel. He continued to explain the plan. "When we get back to Port Alexandra, we will walk along the river and meet my father and his army. There we will organize ourselves for the battle against the Dark Prince. Hannah will alert her father of our approaching army and convince her father that his best strategy would be for him to go out and conquer us once and for all."

"I take it that you are giving an impression of a small army," said Hannah.

"Yes, that is our strategy."

Pavel looked at Cham, as did everyone else. "Are you in?"

Cham slowly nodded her head. "I'm in," she said, with a serious voice. "Business has been slower since he's been in power."

"But you do want to do it for Raja and her mother as well, don't you?" asked Pavel, with a questioning look.

The captain's look remained serious. "Aye I do. And I will fight t' win this battle."

"And your crew?" asked Raja.

"I will talk t' them."

"Your good status can be reestablished in Kazan for doing this," said Raja. "I hope that you take it." The pirate captain said nothing, but Raja could tell she was thinking about it. Raja then turned to Shamra. "How are you feeling?"

"Like I'm in a dream. You and Hannah look so much alike."

"We know," said Hannah, "and it certainly fooled everyone at the palace."

"That's amazing," said Shamra. "You are definitely a good spy."

"Thanks," said Hannah.

Pavel looked at Fedor, who was playing with his sling. He still had his round rock that Cham had found for him. "Where did you get this sling?"

"Cham helped me make it."

Pavel looked surprised. "It looks like a well-made sling."

Fedor proudly held it up for everyone to see. He stood and demonstrated his twirling technique.

"I have t' admit making' the slim' with Fedor was enjoyable. Have you gotten good at it Fedor?" asked Cham.

Fedor nodded. "I practiced on the island, and then Jafar helped me practice at Dragomir Palace."

Pavel wondered how he managed to practice with the crown prince.

"You should practice some more," said Pavel. "When we meet up with my father, you can practice with me."

Fedor's face lit up. "Okay," he said.

Pavel patted Fedor on the back. "And practice good and hard."

Fedor agreed.

During the rest of the trip, Raja, Shamra, and Fedor talked about what it was like in Dragomir Palace and how they had all escaped. A few thoughts had slipped through Raja's mind about Jafar and how he might be feeling about her sudden disappearance. The people of the palace must have been in a panic. The pirates kept a constant look out for anyone following them, but no other ship was seen.

The conversation that was held in the aftercastle of Cham's ship was later recorded in the *Book of Records.* It being the first conversation recorded, they named it the *Meeting of Orsus.*

Chapter 39

The Battle

Cham made sure she sailed her ship into Port Alexandra at night. The Kazan Castle was located along the Volga River, so there was little chance of the ship being noticed. After the ship docked, everyone disembarked, with Hannah departing from the group and making her way to Kazan Castle. She would wait at the wooden city gates early in the morning to be let in by a guard. Her lady-in-waiting, who had been covering for her while she was gone, had secretly arranged this agreement.

Cham had convinced her pirates, who were on the ship, to fight in the battle, and among them were Ivan and Yev. They grouped together as they started walking along the shores of the Kazanka River toward the Volga. They eventually would have to pass the Kazan Castle along the Volga River, but the castle was in a bit from the shore and there were cliffs and steep rocky terrain that could hide them.

The group walked along the shore for half of the night and then slept a little. When it was light, they continued their trek and walked for another two days. They finally reached Viktor's camp. Raja couldn't believe how many people were there. Tents were strewn everywhere, and large numbers of horses were grazing in the fields.

Viktor welcomed Raja with open arms. He had truly been agonized over her disappearance. Raja introduced Shamra and Fedor, and everyone gathered to have a meal. Viktor took the lead.

"We, the Zurkians, will win this battle!" he shouted.

Everyone cheered.

"We will show no fear!"

They all cheered again.

"We will take back the throne!"

The group stood up and cheered even louder.

Viktor went on to explain the plan. "Everyone will leave at the first of dawn. When we are closer to the battlefield, the reinforcements will stay hidden behind the hill. Arhip will lead the reinforcements, who will be riding on horses, and Captain Cham will lead the ground forces. The rest of us will continue over the hill and meet the enemy."

Viktor walked to Pavel and raised his arm. "Pavel at my right." Viktor did the same to Raja. "Raja at my left." Raja and Pavel stood beside Viktor. Joining hands and holding their arms up, Viktor shouted, "Prepare to battle!"

"Prepare to battle!" shouted the crowd.

Raja's eyes swept over the crowd and tingles came to her body. The energy from their loud cheering surged through her. A new power of bravery resonated within her spirit. She herself was ready to battle for the throne of Zurkia.

The next morning came quickly. Shamra was part of the group that would be hiding behind the hill. It was decided that Fedor would ride on the back of Boris' horse, and that they, too, would come in later. The pirates and most of the peasants were assigned to the reinforcement army.

Everything so far was going as planned. Viktor led his army of guards and knights toward Kazan Castle. When close enough, he had his army line up on the battlefield. The enemy army, which had been approaching, did the same. They had come from Bolger Castle, travelling along the Kazanka River, which would have been a three-day journey. The two armies were at a fair play in terms of energy spent in travel and they now faced each other.

Raja, Pavel, and Viktor moved their horses forward and away from the line.

The Dark Prince, who was riding a black horse and wearing a black cape over his armor, came forward from his line. Hannah also came forward and stood her white horse beside her father. She was wearing Raja's green-emerald crown jewel. A third rider, who was the Grand Padesha Tzoycha, sat on another white horse beside the prince. The Dark Prince's army consisted of the Odyhun legionnaires and the Tyhet warriors and definitely outnumbered Viktor's own army. The chieftain was also among the warriors. They were mostly all riding on white horses.

Of course, Viktor's smaller army was part of his strategy, but admittedly he knew he was taking a risk. Viktor had put a lot of time and energy into training his knights, so he also knew that they were strong and that was one of his advantages.

Viktor was the first to speak. He raised his flag. "We have come here because you have stolen the throne."

The Dark Prince shouted back, "No, I am the rightful tzar, and my daughter is the rightful Princess of Kazan. See, my daughter now wears the crown jewel. We will defeat you with our army!"

"You do not tell the truth!" yelled Viktor. "Do you surrender, or do you fight?"

Before the prince could respond, Hannah moved her horse to the center of the battlefield. She shouted, "I surrender, and I join Viktor's army. Raja is the rightful princess of this jewel!"

Hannah took off the crown jewel, rode over to Raja, and draped it around her neck.

The Dark Prince was outraged that his daughter would betray him. He raised his flag and shouted, "We will not surrender!"

Viktor raised his own flag and shouted, "Urra!"

The two armies charged toward one another. Knights and guards were knocked from their horses. In a very short time, some were already injured or killed. The reinforcement army was charging down the crest of the hill. Some had horses and some were on foot, carrying weapons of all sorts. Boris and Fedor were in the lead on their horse. It seemed that the prince's army was winning.

Viktor was in a battle with the padesha and was losing strength with a puncture wound. Pavel saw his father's trouble and quickly moved to help him. The padesha raised his arm again to strike Viktor with his war hammer, and it was at that moment that an arrow struck the padesha from the side. Pavel looked up to see Hannah on her horse with her bow and arrow. The padesha fell. It was enough to keep him on the ground, and Pavel was able to carry his wounded father out of the battle area.

Raja was fighting with her lance and shield, defeating the enemy knights from on top of her horse and skillfully blocking the blows that came against her. But, a powerful thrust of a lance came from behind her and she was knocked down from her horse. It was the Dark Prince. He jumped from his horse and pointed his sword at her. Raja quickly got up and took a fighting position. She was ready to battle.

"I want the honor of doing away with you!" shouted the Dark Prince.

Raja shouted back. "Try as you will, but you won't succeed!"

The two immersed themselves in a harrowing battle. He overpowered Raja and knocked the sword from her hand. Then he hit her hard from the side, and she fell to the ground. Thoughts that she would soon take her last breath shot through her mind. Her situation seemed hopeless.

At that moment, the horses from the reinforcement army entered the battlefield. Fedor and Boris were in the lead. Boris' keen eyes spotted Raja.

"Raja's in trouble!" screamed Boris.

The Dark Prince leaned over Raja. He yelled at her, "Before you die I will take your emerald! It belongs to Hannah!" The jewel was all that he could think of in those few moments. He prepared to grab it from her neck.

At that very instant, Fedor put his round rock in his sling and aimed at the prince. His rock hit the Dark Prince in the face and stunned him. And in the next second, Pavel came up and knocked the prince to the ground with his sword.

"Surrender or die," said Pavel, as he held his sword to the chest of the Dark Prince. When the prince said nothing, Pavel forced his sword harder.

Not wanting to die, the prince spat out his words, "I surrender." Then he screamed, "Halt your fighting!"

Just then, the rest of the reinforcement army that was on foot came surging in on the enemy. The enemy, seeing that they had no chance and that their prince was captured, gave up and retreated.

Viktor, who was still alive, forced himself up with his sword. He staggered through the remaining injured and dead, one of them being the padesha, who was in pain but still alive. There was no grief in Viktor over the padesha's injury, as at the manor he had threatened his son's life and had sought to steal Raja.

Breathing heavily, Viktor now towered over the Dark Prince, who was pinned to the ground with Pavel's sword. Viktor thrust his own sword at the prince. Raja got up from the ground and stood beside Pavel.

"Prepare to meet your death!" said Viktor, trembling with rage. "You've had your last chance for your evil schemes."

Viktor raised his sword to plunge it into the prince.

"No!" shouted Raja. She blocked Viktor's sword with her own sword. "I can't let you do that. He is Hannah's father. Let him live."

Viktor, still trembling, pressed his sword against Raja's sword.

"Put it down!" shouted Raja.

Viktor locked eyes with Raja. Her confident gaze compelled him to obey her order and he slowly brought down his sword. Raja kept her double-edged sword in front of her and stared at Viktor. Her determined look told Viktor that she would not give up until he fully relented. He threw his sword on the ground, but he still wanted to have the last word. In a stern voice, and grimacing from his injury, he spat out his words at the Dark Prince.

"Move yourself and your followers farther north. You are banished from Bolger Castle, which is now no longer your castle. Never set foot in this region again. If it weren't for Raja's kindness, you would be dead by now. Go and never return!"

The Dark Prince slowly rose to his feet, blood smeared over his face from the injury of the stone. He reached for his sword but Raja stopped him, putting her boot on the weapon. The prince looked into Raja's face with a scowl.

"Go without your weapon!"

The prince relented and walked out of the battlefield, past the injured, unable to do anything about them as his army had already fled.

Raja saw the stone that had hit the prince and picked it up. She threw it to Fedor, who was standing not too far away. Fedor caught the stone.

"Keep it as a memory of your bravery!" said Raja. She felt proud of Fedor for fighting in the battle as he did. He was losing his child-like behaviors and becoming more like a young man.

The first thing that now came to Raja's mind was her mother. She hurried toward the city gates, but along the way she stopped to give help to several warriors with bleeding injuries.

By the time Raja reached the gates all the warriors and legionnaires had already surrendered to Viktor's army and had fled. Any others inside the castle who were in alliance with the Dark Prince had already escaped. Viktor was not far behind and was being taken into the castle for immediate attention. He was weak but he would live.

Arhip had led his army with bravery and tact, and fortunately, he, Shamra, Fedor, and Boris had managed to avoid injuries. Pavel was also still standing strong, but was dealing with emotional turmoil. He had not liked the battle, but it seemed it was the only way to save the tzarina. If only there was a different way to bring about what was right other than fighting in a battle. Thankfully, it had not been a long battle, with only a few deaths and some captured warriors and legionnaires.

Hannah had followed Raja and the two met just outside the gates. They both hurried into the Kazan Castle and to the dungeon below. They found the tzarina sitting on the cold stone floor with her head against the wall and her arms resting on her knees. She looked pale and worn. She was extremely weak, but still managed an expression of both relief and surprise when she saw the girls.

Raja ran to her mother's side and knelt down next to her, feeling like she could not even speak. Raja was so happy that her mother was alive, but at the same time felt pain that she was suffering. "Mother, it is truly I. The Dark Prince deceived you with my cousin. Please forgive her."

"Yes, please forgive me, tzarina," said Hannah, with great sincerity. "I had to betray you in order to win your throne back. But I made sure that your life was preserved."

The tzarina listened but was a bit confused. "Am I being freed?"

"Yes," said both girls, at once, as they extended their hands to help the tzarina to her feet. She put her hands against the wall to keep her balance. The girls helped to steady her. The tzarina looked at the girls.

"I'm truly your daughter," said Raja. "And this is my cousin."

"How can I be sure?" asked the tzarina.

Raja uncovered a birthmark that was hidden at the back of her neck.

"Yes, you are Chamaris," said her mother, hugging her and crying at the same time.

Raja hugged her mother back. She was so thankful to finally be with her. She hadn't expected it to be this way, but now it didn't matter anymore. They had the future to look forward to.

Appreciating the moment, but not wanting to stay in the dungeon any longer, Hannah said, “Let’s get out of here. I’m sure we can find a more comfortable place.”

The tzarina looked at Hannah. “I forgive you.”

Hannah bowed very respectfully. The three left the dungeon and went into the chambers of the castle. Every effort was made to quickly restore the tzarina’s health.

Chapter 40

Meant to Be

The throne of Zurkia was secured. Fully recovered, the tzarina resumed her duties and worked to reverse the burden on the peasants that the Dark Prince had created. Raja thought she made a wonderful tzarina and admired her leadership. She indeed sat beautifully on the throne, with her golden red hair and hazel eyes, just as Raja had imagined. Raja's dream to be reunited with her mother had finally come true.

The tzarina was just as proud of her daughter, and she allowed her to keep her name, Raja. In the next few days, Raja was anointed as Princess of Kazan. The tzarina herself felt like a dream had come true. She could actually be with Raja and show motherly love to her. What more happiness could she want? Her prayers had been answered with the silk scarf, and to see Raja wearing it after all these years brought overwhelming joy to her heart. To say the least, the mother and daughter reunion was wonderful and celebrations were being planned.

Of course, two of the invited guests were Shamra and Fedor. But along with them was Shamra's aunt, whom they had found in Kazan Village and had brought to the castle. This was more reason to celebrate, because after much discussion with Shamra's aunt it was found that Shamra and Fedor were brother and sister, which stood to reason, as they certainly looked alike. All three of them were invited to live in the castle as compensation for all the emotional turmoil the aunt had suffered.

Antom received special recognition, as he had been the first one to encounter Cham and her men. Cham's party had bought horses from a farmer in Kazan Village and they had ridden west along the shore toward the manor. Antom, who had just come from the manor, was on a trek to the village when he saw Cham entering the estate and he was brave enough to confront her. It was rare to see a pirate in that part of the country, and it would cause fear and suspicion, but Antom wanted to turn over every stone in his hope that Raja, who was like his own daughter, would be found. Antom had sensed that Cham's intentions were honorable and trustworthy, and he had been the one to notify Pavel at the manor.

Cham was also invited to the celebrations, and because a lot of talk was going on about Kuzma, it was shortly discovered that Cham was Kuzma's daughter. During the voyage back to Zurkia, Cham had realized Kuzma was her father after overhearing a discussion about him, but emotion over the ordeal had kept her from saying anything about it. But further evidence from Fedor and Raja about Kuzma had clarified to everyone that Kuzma indeed was Cham's father. After all, who else would like Chamomile tea and name his daughter Chamomile? In the end, the captain vowed she would one day get her father back.

After everything Raja had seen from Cham, she had no doubt that she would get her father back. She and Cham continued to have some good discussions about the past and how it had influenced her to turn to a life of piracy. She sensed Cham was changing her point of view on life.

Not to neglect the tzarina, Raja was enjoying their long walks together. They laughed and cried and then listened and talked, mostly about love, compassion, and justice. Her mother knew that eventually there would have to be an end to slavery in the Land of Rousse. Her own daughter had been caught in it. It wasn't right. She could not change everything at once, but she would work toward it.

Raja sat at the edge of the cliff by the Kazan Castle, overlooking the Volga River. Wearing her scarf of silk, and the emerald crown jewel from her mother, she held her doll in her hands. The hole in the doll had been stitched. It was a bit frayed on the edge, but Raja thought it still looked as beautiful as ever. Her precious gifts had worked to both free her and save her life.

Raja was still deep in thought when Pavel came over and sat beside her. "It's good to be back, isn't it?"

"Yes, indeed, nothing short of a miracle."

"What do you think brought it about?" asked Pavel.

"Love and hope."

"I've no doubt about that."

Raja looked at Pavel. "Where there is love, there is forgiveness, where there is forgiveness, there is redemption."

"I couldn't have said it better," said Pavel. "And so did you hear about Cham?"

"No. What's going on with her?"

"Your tzarina mother awarded her a large sum of coin for helping with your rescue and for fighting in the battle."

"That's a change from having to steal it," said Raja.

"I agree, but get this. Your mother also gave her the red ruby."

"That's amusing," said Raja.

"And what's more is that Cham said she is going to sell it back to Dracon."

"Well, that is even more amusing," said Raja.

"I agree; like I said, things can get around."

Raja and Pavel laughed over the circumstances of the crown jewel.

"What does Cham want to use her fortune for?"

"She wants to use the coin to convert her village into honest working people. She says they will still retain their fighting skills, but now use it against evil instead of for evil."

Raja's face beamed. "Amazing! That sounds like she's redeeming herself."

Pavel saw the joy in Raja's face. "I knew you'd be happy about the news. She even looks different. She's changing from the inside out."

"A joy to know," said Raja.

"Indeed."

"I suppose Ivan and Yev have decided to stay there."

"They have, and she will need all the help she can get because when they turn good, evil will pursue them. It's often the case."

Raja thought about the comment and agreed with it.

"Changing the subject, do you know what is happening with Hannah?" asked Pavel.

"Yes, she's moving back to Bolger Castle. My mother has anointed her as Princess of Bolger."

"That's great," said Pavel. "I admire her for taking on that duty."

"Me, too."

"What about you? What are you going to be doing?"

Raja smiled at Pavel. "Oh, you know what I'm doing. I'll be back at the manor just after winter."

"Just checking." Pavel smiled, trying not to seem too eager for the time to come. "I can see that you'll want to spend some time with your tzarina mother."

"That's true," said Raja. "Thank you for understanding, but I will be looking forward to seeing everyone at the manor again."

"Good to hear," said Pavel.

"Let's go and help my mother with the celebrations," said Raja.

"At your command," said Pavel with a serious face as he got up and bowed low to the ground.

"You are a joker," said Raja with hands on her hips. "Race you to the castle."

"As you wish!"

CPSIA information can be obtained
at www.ICGtesting.com
Printed in the USA
LVHW040723081221
705576LV00003B/279